JULIE
AND THE
PHANTOMS
Whatever Happens

D0059329

JULIE AND THE PHANTOMS

Whatever Happens

An Original Novel by

Candace Buford

Scholastic Inc.

To Little C, for helping me remember. —C. B.

1

Julie

Luke, Reggie, and Alex were always real to me, even when I was the only one who could see them. And when I discovered they were visible to other living people when we played music together, that felt real, too—better than real. When Reggie plucked his bass strings, Alex wailed on the drums, and Luke strummed his guitar as he sang along with me and my piano—it felt like a dream come true to play with my phantoms, to bring our music to life.

But *come on*, they're ghosts—or *musician spirits*, to use Alex's preferred term. Even though they felt real, they were still just made of air. They always faded away at the end of a song, and I expected nothing less tonight.

But tonight was *different*.

My eyes snapped open as I pulled away from my

hug with Luke. I gripped his hands, feeling his skin push back. "How can I feel you?"

"I—I don't know." He scrunched up his face, shaking his head.

I grabbed his face between both hands, my eyes growing wider when my hands didn't slide right through his ghostly form. Luke was very much *solid*. He felt real to me—literally.

This can't be happening.

Playing our show at the famous Orpheum Theater in Hollywood was supposed to be Luke, Reggie, and Alex's unfinished business—their second chance at the show they never got to play before they died. And it was their best bet at crossing over before Caleb Covington's curse zapped them into nothing—or into an eternity of being forced to play in the Hollywood Ghost Club's house band. So why were the guys still here instead of over on the other side, wherever that was?

I rubbed my forehead, wondering if I was still riding the high of our performance tonight. We'd *killed* it at the Orpheum. Our chemistry was electric, and it had radiated toward the crowd like the rays of the sun. Everywhere our music touched, it brightened the crowd's faces. And right now Luke's face was glowing, with the pulse of *life*. Had our beats been so powerful that they resurrected him from the dead?

Don't be ridiculous, Jules. You can't just bring someone back from the dead!

But stranger things had happened lately.

"I feel stronger." Luke gripped my hands tighter, and a tear slipped down his cheek.

"Alex, Reggie, come," I said over his shoulder, where our bandmates looked on in disbelief. I waved them over to where we were standing. I wanted to see if they were solid, too. If whatever was happening to Luke—whatever *I* was doing?—would happen to them.

They rushed across the garage studio with their arms open, smashing into us in a giant group hug. When we pulled away from each other, the purple stamps on their wrists detached and floated above our heads, disappearing into thin air.

"What do you think that means?" I asked, my eyebrows knitting together. I hoped it was the last we'd see of Caleb and his Hollywood Ghost Club.

"I think *the band's back*." Luke's eyes glowed with hope.

"Can we try that hug thing again?" Alex asked, pulling us into another group hug with his long, gangly arms.

I pawed Reggie's tuxedo, feeling the silkiness beneath my fingers. Then I pinched Alex's arm to confirm he was solid, too.

"Ouch!" He frowned for a second, but his scowl quickly perked into a smile. He laughed, like he welcomed the pain. "I felt that. *Ow!*"

"Just double-checking." I chuckled into our group hug. I was about to do the same thing to Reggie, but he wriggled free.

"Well, I think this means it's time to *eat*." He patted his stomach, his eyes bright. "Do you think that burger place on Sunset Boulevard is still open?"

I stared at him, unable to blink. I could *not* believe Reggie's first thought was about fast food. How could he think about burgers at a time like this?

"What? I haven't eaten real, non-ghost food in twenty-five years. I'm *starving*." He slicked his dark hair away from his forehead. "Who's with me?" Then he balled his hands into fists and squeezed his eyes shut.

"Wait," Alex said, holding a hand up.

Reggie pried one eye open, clearly annoyed with the delay.

"Aren't we going to talk about this crazy awesome thing that's happening to us?" Alex reached out and poked my arm, feeling solid flesh. "I mean, is Julie the only one we can touch, or are we solid to everyone? And if we're solid right now, does that mean other people can *see* us, too?"

"Any theories?" I crossed my arms, searching Luke's face. I knew he probably didn't have all the answers, but a girl could hope.

"I don't know." He shook his head.

"May I suggest we find out at the burger place?" Reggie raised his eyebrows.

Alex dismissed him with a grumble. "You *still* might not be able to eat."

Then he paused. "Wait—Willie. Can he still see me? Is he even okay after everything that happened with Caleb tonight?" Alex's face grew worried as he thought about his crush. From what he'd told me, Willie was a seriously cute skateboarder ghost who could skate wherever he wanted now that he was dead. He and Alex had their own unfinished business to take care of, but it was unclear if that could be resolved right now. If Alex was solid to *me*, maybe he wouldn't be to other ghosts like Willie. The guys were definitely in a weird gray area at the moment.

But my phantoms had never really played by the rules. They were special.

"Dude, we can go look for him if you want." Reggie

said, softening his stance. He may have been eager to test the limits of their current solidness, but that didn't take precedence over Alex's more pressing concerns.

"Uh, thanks, Reggie." Alex looked touched as he nudged Reggie's arm. He couldn't hide the blush pooling under his cheeks, and Alex divined *exactly* what was still on his mind. "Yes, fine. And then we can go try to eat burgers."

"If you insist," he said, his eyes bright. Reggie turned to me and Luke. "You guys want to come out with us?"

"I think—" Luke looked at me, raising his eyebrow. It was a question, asking if I wanted to stay or go.

Part of me wanted to stay with my bandmates and celebrate all night. We'd played the Orpheum, ditched Caleb, and the guys and I could *hug*—at least for now. I was torn between hanging with the group and spending some alone time with Luke. But one look at Luke's intense gaze was all it took. I *definitely* wanted to stay.

"I think we're good here," I said, feeling a blush creep across my face.

"*Uh-huh.*" Reggie smirked at me before elbowing Alex in the side. "You ready to go?"

Alex hesitated and exhaled in a rush, and Reggie rolled his eyes. "Oh, come on, Alex. You're not scared, are you? Poofing is like second nature."

"Well, yeah, but that was before Julie could touch us." He reached his arm out and poked my elbow with his pinkie, then shook his head. "See? What if we *can't* poof anymore?"

"Let's find out," Reggie said with a grin. Then he instantly poofed out of the room.

"Okay." Alex held his chest, relief relaxing his facial features. He gave us a little wave and wiggled his eyebrows. "See you two later."

And with a *poof,* he was gone.

I blinked rapidly, my breath hitching as Alex and Reggie disappeared before my eyes. It was nothing new to me—I'd seen them poof away dozens of times before. But it also *was* new, because now they were solid. Or, at least, I could touch them.

What did this mean for the rest of their ghostly abilities?

I had so many questions about the guys' current solid state, but one look at Luke and my mind went blank. *Poof*—my questions vanished, just like Alex and Reggie had.

A weird stillness fell over the studio, and I could only hear Luke's shuffling feet mixed with my own nervous heartbeat. We'd been alone together countless times, staying up late writing songs and talking. But for some reason, right now, I was nervous to be so close to him.

"So." I tucked a bundle of curls behind my ear and stepped toward my mom's old piano, putting space between me and the crackling energy buzzing around Luke.

"So," he said with a cautious grin.

I'd had crushes before, but none as strong as the one I had on Luke. And right now, as my heart hammered against my chest, my feelings for him had reached new depths. I'd never felt like this before. *Never.*

Flynn liked to tease me that I had it bad for a *ghost*, and she was one hundred percent right. The whole "being dead" thing aside, Luke was kinda my dream guy, and right now he was staring at me with a mix of wonder and awe. By some stroke of luck, I think Luke liked me, too.

His gazed locked with mine, and for a second I thought he might say something more, but his eyelashes fluttered and he looked away.

Omigod, I can't!

My stomach churned, a swarm of a gazillion butterflies. When I looked up, Luke had stepped closer. He laid a hand on the piano, close to mine.

"You were *incredible* tonight," I said, my voice a little shaky.

"Are you kidding me? You *crushed* it." He hiked up one white sneaker on the piano bench and ran his fingers across the ivory keys, smiling at every solid touch. "You literally hopped across the stage when you saw me poof in and start playing."

A small laugh escaped my lips as I remembered the excitement I'd felt when Luke finally appeared onstage. He'd flickered in and out, and I wasn't sure he'd make it. But he'd stood tall at the microphone, as if he were willing himself to stay here, with us. With me.

"I didn't know what had happened to you guys," I said, my voice lowering to little more than a whisper. "When you didn't show up for the pre-show, I figured you'd moved on—or just stopped existing."

After my dad drove me to the Orpheum and dropped me off backstage (he had VIP credentials and absolutely *loved* his ability to roam the place freely), Flynn and I had waited almost an hour for the guys to show up. Alex, Reggie, and Luke never appeared backstage, and I'd been sure they had disappeared for good.

"I almost left," I said in a smaller voice.

I remembered running out of the venue's side door, ready to never look back. Crying into the dark and dingy alley, I'd called out to my mom—for help or comfort, anything. And then, out of nowhere, a woman had walked by with a bouquet of red dahlias and given me one. It was my mom's favorite flower. It was obviously a sign from her, right?

It *had* to be.

"I'm glad you stayed. We were stuck with Caleb. He forced us to join his band onstage, and we literally *couldn't* stop playing our instruments. He had some sort of weird, freaky hold on us." Luke shook his head. "It took every ounce of my energy to get to the Orpheum."

"The important thing is that you *did* come back. Even if it wasn't your unfinished business, you couldn't miss out on playing there again."

"That's not why I came back, and you know it." Luke breathed deeply before sliding his hand across the piano's surface.

Our fingers grazed, and even though the contact was brief, I felt a jolt of energy rush through me. My heart raced against my chest.

"You felt that, too, right?" Luke asked with an inquisitive eyebrow raised. And I wasn't sure if he was referring to the jolt of electricity that pricked my fingers or the general awesomeness of the night.

"Um, *yeah*," I responded to both of those possibilities. I collapsed onto a pile of throw pillows on the floor, my legs too wobbly to support me any longer. "There aren't many perfect days like today."

"Yeah, there's only one other time I remember feeling like this—when I was at an all-time high, buzzing about the future and whatever came next," he said, joining me on the floor. He sat cross-legged, just out of reach.

"Me too," I said, nodding slowly, thinking about the last truly perfect day I'd had. I laid my head against a pillow, looking up at the ceiling where my mom and I had hung old chairs, giving them a second life. Of course, that was right before I found out she was sick— bittersweet, but still perfect. "I still remember it like yesterday."

"Tell me about it," Luke said with a playful grin.

"I will," I said, returning his smile. "But you go first."

Luke

I'd like to tell you that I'm *Mr. Responsible*—that the night before the biggest show of my life I'd be tucked in bed, getting a good night's sleep before I hit the stage. But the night before our show at the Orpheum also happened to be the night of the Foo Fighters concert, a gnarly new band started by the drummer of Nirvana. I'd worked double shifts at the diner to afford tickets for me and the boys. My feet were still throbbing from all that time spent leaning over the bussing station.

Not that I was complaining or anything—I was happy to have my part-time gig at the diner. It allowed me enough time for school and official band business, and the owner of the place was generous enough to give me extra hours when I needed the cash, which, since

I'd run away, was more often than not. Food and guitar strings weren't cheap—and neither were concert tickets. Needless to say, this show was a splurge.

But there was no way we'd miss this.

By the end of the show, the Palace Theatre was still packed—and I mean *packed*. The buzz from the crowd flooded my ears. You could almost *feel* the energy around us. I couldn't wait for one of Sunset Curve's shows to feel like this. And I wouldn't have to wait long. Our showcase at the Orpheum was less than twenty-four hours away.

The guitar blared through the venue, hitting our ears before the rest of the crowd's—because, *of course*, Alex, Reggie, Bobby, and I had wiggled our way to the front. The drumbeat hammered with the rhythm of my own heart. I bobbed my head from side to side as the music transported me—right up to the metal gate dividing the audience from the stage. I rocked the divider along with the music, drawing the attention of the nearby security guard.

"What did I tell you about rattling this?" He gripped the railing, his arm muscles bulging as he stilled it.

"All right, all right," I said, holding my hands up in surrender.

"Cool it, Luke." Reggie nudged me with his elbow. "Or next time he's gonna kick you out."

"I mean, would that be so bad? It's already the third encore," Alex said with a yawn. "Maybe it's time for us to head home anyway."

Bobby tugged on my sleeve, thrusting his Casio watch in my face.

"Let's roll!" he yelled over the applause. "We wanna beat the rush to the exits."

"Come on, guys," I protested, turning my attention back to the stage. When I saw Dave Grohl up there, I saw *myself*. I got my best moves from big shows, so I wanted to soak up as much as I could. Was it a good idea to stay up half the night on the eve of your breakout concert? Ehhh—maybe not. But it was *totally* worth it. To feel the energy of a large crowd, to know that that would be me onstage in less than twenty-four hours. Everything fell into place, and I felt like I'd already made it.

Well—*almost* made it. I just had to get some decent sleep. My stomach grumbled. Okay, maybe some street food and *then* a decent night's sleep.

"Fine." I pushed my bandmates into the aisle and pointed toward the side exit. My stomach grumbled again when we hit the pavement outside. "Boys, who's up for a quick bite?" I asked.

"I'm starving," Reggie said. He clapped his hands as he spun around, walking backward so that he could face us. Reggie took his meals very seriously, which was why he ate about seven times a day.

"You're *always* hungry," Bobby said with an eye roll. It earned him one of Reggie's playful punches to the shoulder.

We rounded the corner, and that's when I saw *her* car—the 1977 Volvo station wagon, its turquoise coloring barely visible under the dim streetlights. I drew in a sharp breath, then shrank back behind the alley wall. Reggie scrunched his face up, looking to Alex in confusion. But Bobby stepped forward, meeting me in my makeshift hiding spot.

"You're looking at the Volvo over there, aren't you?" He flicked his head toward the street.

I nodded, poking my head out to catch another glimpse of my family's car. Well, at least it *looked* like our car. Bobby nodded slowly, understanding where my anxiety was coming from.

"That's not her, dude." He patted my shoulder, gripping it reassuringly.

"Who are we talking about?" Reggie asked, a little slow on the uptake.

"Luke's mom, obviously." Alex bopped Reggie on the backside of his head.

Bobby swallowed hard and turned back to Luke.

"Just think about it—why would she be all the way out here at"—he held his watch up to his sleepy eyes—"almost one in the morning?"

The rational side of me knew he was right. My mom didn't leave the house after 8:00 p.m., let alone wander around on this side of the 101 freeway, so far from home. But every time I saw a station wagon that looked remotely like hers I *freaked*.

I couldn't help it.

Because deep down I wasn't happy with the way we'd left things—the way I'd screamed at her as I packed my bags, the way she looked at me, her face tear-stained and splotchy, the way I'd slammed the door after telling her that I *never ever wanted to see her face again*. I wished I could rewind and handle it differently. My mom and I had unfinished business.

But first I needed to prove to her that I could make a career as a musician—that's the only way we'd ever work things out. Until then, I was fine ducking down alleys to avoid her.

A loud gurgle rippled through the silence. We all turned to Reggie, who shrugged sheepishly.

"Hunger waits for no one." His mouth stretched into his signature goofy grin. Then he nodded toward the food vendor across the road. His nostrils perked up at the smell of street meats, and I had to admit—it smelled delicious.

I hopped up and walked with the guys across the street. They were nice enough not to bring up the station wagon or the fight I'd had with my mom. We usually poked fun at one another about everything, but we all knew which subjects were off-limits.

"So, are you sleeping at the studio again?" Reggie asked.

"What other choice do I have?" I shrugged, stepping onto the sidewalk. Storming out of my house meant I technically didn't have a bedroom anymore. I'd used the couch at the studio on and off for the past few months, hoping the owners didn't think I was *living* there. We only rented the space for band practice, not as an apartment. Underage kids couldn't rent apartments.

Believe me, I've tried.

As if he could read the worry painted on my face, Alex slung his arm around my shoulders and offered me exactly what I needed.

"I've got an open bunk, if you want it."

"Thanks, Alex." I smiled, then stepped forward to order my food. I groaned when I read the menu prices. These hot dogs were more than twice the cost at our usual joint—Sam 'N' Ella's Dogs. I hesitated, my fingers hovering over the few dollar bills left in my wallet.

"Come on. Live a little!" Reggie laughed from behind me.

Reluctantly, I handed the guy at the register the rest of my cash. I figured we'd be famous after our show at the Orpheum. By this time tomorrow we could have an agent—maybe even a record deal! Why not start living large now?

"Seriously, we gotta take these on the road," Alex said between bites. "I need sleep *real* bad."

"We can sleep when we're dead." I chuckled, wondering if any of us would really be able to sleep tonight anyway—the eve of the most important day of our lives. I shrugged, stuffing a hot dog in my face. It didn't have the same rustic taste as our usual dogs—there was something about Sam 'N' Ella's that left a tang in my mouth. But I didn't really care how it tasted, as long as it hit the spot.

We huddled together, the sound of chewing filling the air. This might be one of the last times we ate street meat together; we were rising stars, after all. Our showcase at the Orpheum would surely catapult us to stardom, and pretty soon I'd be buying steak dinners for everyone.

"Cheers to the future!" I raised my half-eaten hot dog over my head. The guys raised what was left of their own food, joining me in a toast to our inevitable success.

"Tomorrow we're going to be legends."

Julie

Carrie wasn't exactly dead to me, but I could feel our friendship flatlining. For the life of me, I could not figure out what was going on. She'd been super cold and flaky since before school started, and I wasn't sure why. My best friend, Flynn, would *never* treat me like this. In fact, I couldn't remember anyone ghosting me the way Carrie had. *Seriously*, this silent treatment was starting to worry me. Before I knew it, I was flipping through her social media.

Yeah, yeah. I know I'm super lame.

But I was too curious to see what she was up to. Maybe she was still having a rough time at home. Her parents were going through a divorce, and as tough as Carrie tried to be, I knew she was hurting.

I scrolled through her recent posts online, gritting

my teeth as I saw the time stamp on the bottom of her latest duck-faced selfie. It was taken an hour ago, right around the time I texted her about maybe hanging out and going shopping. She'd obviously seen my message and was ignoring me on purpose. *Ouch.*

I don't know why I did it, but I scrolled down to the next picture. I bit my tongue when I saw Carrie making that same selfie face with Nick. *Double ouch.*

She *knew* I had a crush on Nick. I'd fallen for him the moment I heard him play one of Trevor Wilson's soulful ballads on his guitar. The way his eyes closed as he strummed the song by one of my favorite musicians—I was all in. Carrie was crossing a line.

I lay back against my pillow, crossing my arms over my chest as I gazed at the ceiling. My heart ached, and it wasn't just because Nick was posing for pics with another girl. The true wound came from my crumbling friendship with Carrie. I had a sneaking suspicion that I was losing a really good friend, and I felt helpless to stop it. It was pretty heartbreaking.

My thumbs rapidly tapped against my phone screen as I texted Flynn, asking her if she could hang out later. As my best bud since the first grade, she had a way of talking me down, whirling me into one of her many distractions instead of letting me dwell on the heavy. I didn't have to worry about hearing back from Flynn—she was always there for me. I shoved my phone into my pocket, knowing she'd respond soon.

In the meantime, there was only one person I wanted to run to right now, and that was my mom.

I scampered down the stairs of my house and made a detour to the kitchen island, where a basket of fruit sat on the counter. I nabbed a banana and peeled the skin back as I nudged the back door open.

The wind hit me with a *whoosh*, cooling my clammy forehead as I made a beeline to the garage studio. Taking the stone steps two at a time, my mom's piano music grew louder with each stride. I peeked through the dusty window and watched her play the sheet music for her student, who sat beside her, turning the pages as she struck the keys with ease.

"You really have to play it more allegro when you come out of the bridge section here." Mom pointed to the sheet resting on the stand. "Practice it just like I showed you, and we'll revisit it next week."

After some rustling of papers and the sound of a backpack being zipped up, the door to the garage studio swung open. I scooted to the side to allow the student to get by, apologizing under my breath for being in the way.

"I thought I heard you out there," Mom called from inside.

"I just like listening to you, that's all." I crossed the threshold, sidling up to her as she cleared the piano of her lesson plans.

"You can do better than *listen*. You can come play." Mom slid a few familiar pages from her personal notebook forward, wiggling them in front of my face—tempting me to see what she'd added to our latest creation.

"Are you done for the day? Don't you have another lesson?" It was Saturday morning. My mom *always* had lessons lined up, especially on the weekends. As one of the best music theory teachers and private tutors in central LA—a city known for its music scene—Rose Molina was in high demand.

"I had a last-minute cancellation." She shrugged, arranging the pages on the piano.

"That's rude," I grumbled under my breath. Okay—maybe I was still a little sore from Carrie giving me the cold shoulder. But you can't just cancel on people and not care about their feelings! Not when you've been best friends since you were kids. I deserved more than that—especially from Carrie.

Okay, Jules. Just breathe.

"Sometimes you gotta just let it go, mija. Water off a duck's back, right?" She gripped my chin, tilting it upward so that I could meet her gaze. Her soft brown eyes melted away my lingering frustrations, and I quickly forgot about Carrie. Mom patted the seat next to her. "Ven, how about we take another stab at our song?"

My mom's slender fingers started playing the notes to our newest work-in-progress. She nodded at me, inviting me to sing with her.

> Don't blink
> No, I don't want to miss it
> One thing
> And it's back to the beginning
> 'Cause everything is rushing in fast
> Keep going on, never look back

Her hands slowed as her fingers trailed off the piano keys. This was as far as we'd gotten last week—the song was still working its way out of our minds.

"I keep kicking around this line about floating in the air." I tilted my head to the side, trying to see if I could make it fit into this song.

"Floating in the air." My mom began playing the piano in an upbeat allegro. *"Just like a chair."*

Her hand faltered on the keys as she burst into giggles. I couldn't help but laugh, too.

"Okay, maybe we'll save that line for another song." My shoulders rumbled through another laugh. "Besides, a chair can't float in the air."

"Of course it can. Haven't I told you that anything is possible if you put your mind to it?" She smiled at me, and then her look grew distant, like it did when she thought of the perfect combination of music and lyrics.

She slipped a pencil from behind her ear and jotted down a few more lines. This was how she wrote—in the moment, dropping everything she was doing to chase the song.

"I think I've got the next verse," she said, her fingers gliding over the notes. I scooted closer, looking over her shoulder to read her new addition to the song. Mom lifted her head and sang the new lines:

Right now
I'm loving every minute
Hands down
Can't let myself forget it, no
'Cause everything is rushing in fast
Keep holding on, never look back

"What do you think, mi amor?" she asked, raising an eyebrow as she tapped the keys in a soft melody.

"I love it, but it's still missing something. We need the chorus—the hook." My eyes tightened as I looked at the music sheet, as if the lyrics were hiding behind a treble clef.

"You wanna know what I think? I think this is going to be good enough to debut in Hollywood—maybe at a small theater or music club. There's something special about this one."

"What do *you* know about Hollywood clubs?" I said with a laugh. Thinking about my mom out on the town—in Hollywood of all places—sent another giggle bubbling up in my chest.

"Enough to know that this song and 'Fueling the Fires' and all our other songs are good enough to grace the stage of any open mic night in this city."

"Okay, stop." I rolled my eyes, feeling my cheeks heat. She *had* to say that our songs were good because she was my mom. "Let's just start with singing one at my quinceañera. Leave the Hollywood clubs to the *Hollywood people.*"

"Hey, I used to be one of those young 'Hollywood people.' Up to no good with musicians and handsome photographers." She winked at me, and I knew she was talking about my dad. They'd met a million years ago at some dive on the boulevard. "This new song of ours reminds me a little of a band I met once. They were sort of famous in their time. Well, *almost* famous."

"Are they still around?" I turned in my seat, looking to my mom. She rarely shared about her time as a struggling artist.

But Aunt Victoria chimed in before Mom could answer. "Your mother always was such a sucker for the brooding rocker. And she's got the junk to prove it," Aunt Victoria said from the doorway, looking like she'd just come from a board meeting in her collared shirt and pencil skirt. She lowered her sunglasses and looked over their rim, nodding toward the loft space above the piano.

"Seriously, have you seen the rock-and-roll graveyard up there?" A small smile tugged at her lips as she teased her sister.

Mom chuckled, then yawned deeply.

"Don't tell me you and Ray went out last night, too." Tía folded her arms and pursed of her lips. She was like a second mom to me and my brother. Sometimes she even mothered my mom, too.

"You know our date night is once a month. And it just so happens to be tonight." Mom yawned again, looking like she might not make it until then. "No, I'm just a bit tired today, that's all."

"But it's barely noon," I said, looking at my phone to check the time.

"I think maybe I need more iron or vitamin D or something to kick-start my energy. My doctor is running some blood tests, so we'll see." She ruffled my hair, trying to rattle the frown off my face, but her smile was tight. She smiled wider, erasing her worry lines. "I do miss the days when I could sleep in like your tía."

"No you don't." Tía waved her hand dismissively. A warm smile pulled at her lips as she looked Mom in the eyes. "You always did want to be a mom."

"I did, didn't I?" She nudged me with her elbow before sliding off the piano bench. Gripping Tía's shoulders, she said, "And it'll happen for you, too."

"Ah," Tía moaned, rolling her eyes. She was trying to look like she didn't care, but I could tell that she did. "Anyway, I came for a spa day. Vámonos."

"All right, first order of business: Find Tía some loungewear." Mom raised her eyebrows, nodding toward her not-so-casual attire. She then gestured to her sister's hair. "Come on. Let your hair down."

"Está bien." She flicked her head toward the door. "But only if you curl it like you did last time."

"Deal."

Mom held my hand as she followed Tía out of the studio and up the walkway to our back door. My aunt chatted animatedly about changing up her look— maybe trying something edgier, like borrowing a leather jacket from Mom's rocker days. Mom laughed softly, indulging her sister in her plans for the day.

I was only half present, my mind still wandering through the notes of our new song. My mom's new verse was amazing, of course, but it needed something to bring it all together. I hummed the tune under my breath, determined to find the rest of my lyrics.

But I wasn't in a rush. We had time.

Luke

My shoulder sank into the thin mattress of the bottom bunk, and my eyelids flapped open. My sight was fuzzy from sleep, but my eyes adjusted quickly as I blinked them awake. I squinted at the clock on Alex's desk, which said it was shortly after 7:00 a.m. I rolled onto my back to find Alex's leg dangling from the top bunk, his toe hovering just above my chest. He gripped the railing and dipped down, nudging me with his foot again.

"Okay, I'm up," I said, propping myself up on my elbows. My chest rumbled through a burp, and I tasted some of last night's chili dog. I *definitely* hadn't slept long enough if I could still taste our late-night eats. I collapsed onto my pillow, surrendering to the weight of exhaustion. "Gimme a sec."

We couldn't have slept more than five hours. Alex's offer to crash had rescued me from the nightmare of after-hours bus transit back to the studio and gave me a solid bed to sleep on instead of a lumpy couch. I was super grateful for his kindness, and I fully intended to take advantage of it. I rolled over, prepared to slip in some more snoozing, but Alex wasn't having it. He kicked me awake again.

"Geez! Alex, come on," I said, my voice thick with sleep.

"Would you keep it down?" Alex's eyes grew wide, and he flicked his head toward the bedroom door across the room. "My parents are still sleeping."

"So?" I scrunched my face up.

"Look, I don't want them to hear you and be weird about . . . you know, me having a guy over." He hopped down from his top bunk, his long legs nearly knocking into his desk. "You know the drill."

Ahh. The *drill*. It had been so long since I'd slept over at Alex's house, I'd almost forgotten.

Alex's parents knew me pretty well, so this wouldn't be my first encounter with them. Back in the day, I'd slept over at the Mercer house plenty of times, especially when my mom and I were arguing. But ever since Alex came out to his parents, they were *weird* anytime

Alex brought a guy friend home—like they were worried he had more on his mind than just hanging out with us. It drove Alex crazy.

I didn't blame him. It drove *me* crazy, too, because their treatment of Alex was a downright *buzzkill*.

His parents largely ignored him these days, leaving a strained silence whenever he entered the room. And they weren't exactly supportive of his musical abilities either. They used to be so warm and welcoming, but all that had changed. And their silence and coldness had started to dampen the brightness of Alex's smile.

It really, *really* sucked.

So, now, when any of us came over, we did our own thing, quietly and under the radar of their watchful gaze. And if we happened to fall asleep after watching too much TV and eating too much junk food, we were up early the next morning and gone before his folks could see us and draw some stupid conclusions.

Ugh.

I don't know. It still bugged me—all this dancing around to please parents who would obviously never be pleased. But what did I know about pleasing parents?

"I'll get dressed." I flung the blanket off my legs, hoping to quell Alex's anxiety by making moves. I managed to pry myself off the twin-size mattress, but the top of my head clipped the slats above me. Alex's bunkbeds may have been cool when we were younger but not anymore. I rubbed my head, hoping to dull the sting.

"Thanks, man," Alex said.

"Your parents are being totally bogus," I grumbled as I searched for my shirt.

"I know." He rolled his eyes and chuckled. "It's not like you're even my type."

I gasped, pretending like I was offended. Alex tossed me my jeans, then dug in his closet for his own clothes while I put them on.

I wasn't sure what Alex's type was. But I knew when he finally decided to put himself out there, he was going to bring home a good guy. I just wished I could use his smarts when picking out my own dates.

Who was I kidding?

Dating wasn't really a priority right now. For me, it was all about the music. And we had a show in less than fourteen hours. A surge of adrenaline rushed through my veins.

I finally spotted my shirt beneath the bottom bunk and quickly grabbed it off the floor. I was prepared to pull it over my head, but the stench caught me off guard. I jerked my head back. Yup, I *definitely* needed to do laundry soon. One whiff of that fabric, and I could smell the sweat from the concert venue, the mustiness of the late-night Los Angeles streets, and the body odor of someone who may or may not have showered in a couple days.

Yeah, I can get a little grody. So, sue me.

"I can't wear this." I tossed my shirt across the room, nearly missing Alex's face. His nostrils flared as he caught a whiff of it. He slouched against the edge of his desk, fanning his face with his hand.

"Dude, that is *foul*. I may never smell again." He held his breath as he bent down to retrieve my tank. He pinched the fabric so that he was barely touching it. After dropping it into his hamper, he kicked the lid closed, containing the funk for the time being. "That shirt's in time-out. I can wash it later, but it won't be ready in time for the show."

"Can I borrow one of yours?" I clasped my hands together.

"I've got you covered—*literally*." He laughed to himself. He ran his fingers through his blond hair as he crossed the room to the black dresser and slid open the middle drawer. At random, he selected a shirt, then knocked the drawer shut. He held the white shirt out to me. "Here you go."

I held up the shirt, and I couldn't help but laugh at

the retro band name on the front. "Rush?"

"What?" He scoffed. "They're *legendary*. Their drummer was one of the all-time greats."

"I just thought you were more of a The Who guy, that's all," I said, flinging the shirt over my bare shoulder. "Any chance I can get a shower, too?"

"The one at the studio still acting up?"

"It works when it wants to." I was lucky our garage studio had a rickety old bathroom attached, but the shower had poor water pressure and bad lighting. I'm not complaining—I was seriously grateful to have the studio as my refuge. But sometimes I wanted to experience the trappings of *home*—especially on shower and laundry days.

"Just make it quick." Alex tossed me a towel, then grabbed his bedroom doorknob. "I'm going to go change my laundry so that I can have my lucky shirt in time for the show."

"And we need all the luck we can get today." I rubbed my hands together, eager to get this day started. "Our first interview *and* a show at the Orpheum. Can you believe it?"

Sunset Curve was being interviewed by the music magazine *Spin*—an honor reserved for the hottest up-and-comers. It wasn't a cover or anything, just a small feature in some obscure section of the magazine, but none of that mattered to me. We were *in*. And since we didn't have any professional photos, they had agreed to take our first official band picture—one where we didn't have to use a disposable camera perched on a wobbly stack of books, like we did for our demo. This was the big leagues.

"Hollywood, here we come," Alex said with a grin.

Alex

Poking my head out of my bedroom door, I made sure the coast was clear before darting down the hallway and taking the stairs to the basement. The splashed concrete floors were cold against my bare feet as I scurried to the washing machine. When I opened the lid, I gasped.

Everything was pink. *Pink.*

"How the heck?" I mumbled to myself as I scooped my clothes into the laundry basket. I dug through the damp pile, searching for the culprit. A single red sock unfurled itself from the bundle of formerly white shirts.

Idiot.

I sank to the floor, resting my head against the door to the dryer. I prodded the pile with my finger, taking inventory of the damage. A good chunk of my wardrobe was now drenched in pink—including my go-to Fresh shirt, which I always wore to big shows. My breath escaped in a rush of air.

How could I wear this tonight?

Look, I'm not superstitious or anything—I'm a rational human being who knows that there is no *actual* correlation between my clothing and my good fortune. But I got a kick out of the coincidence of it all, the self-fulfilling prophecy of wearing the same shirt for every big show. Every time I wore it behind my drums, the legend grew more, and my Fresh shirt became luckier.

I turned the shirt over in my hands, looking at its soft pink color. It really didn't look half bad. If I was being honest, I'd always had a thing for pink. I just didn't want *all* my clothes to be that color.

I scraped myself off the floor. I didn't have time to wallow. Today was still going to be great. Tonight, Sunset Curve would become legends.

With the laundry loaded into the dryer, I turned on the heat and headed upstairs. I'd have just enough time to eat a quick breakfast by the time the cycle ended—that would give Luke plenty of time to take his shower. I'd asked him to make it a short one, but I knew he wouldn't. He couldn't help himself. The shower at the studio *was* pretty sad.

But no matter what faults the studio had, it was still our second home.

Honestly? Sometimes it felt like my primary home. I probably spent as much time there as I did at my house these days. The studio didn't have the eerie stillness I felt at home. There was always plenty of noise and music and laughter—the guys made sure of that. And I couldn't wait to meet up with them later today.

I swung the door to my bedroom open, and Luke was leaning against my desk. "That shower was hella fast."

"I couldn't shower, dude," he whispered, gesturing to the door. "Someone else is in the bathroom."

I stood still, listening to the floorboards creak in the hallway. We both held our breaths as we heard the bathroom door open and shut down the hall. I turned slowly to Luke, biting down on both lips. There was only one way out of this situation.

"You're not gonna *love* this idea, but you're gonna do this for me because we are best buds," I said, squinting as I tilted my head to the side.

"What?" he asked warily.

"Go out through the window?" I held my hands up. "It's either that or I'm grounded for the show tonight."

"Alex." Luke sighed, putting his head in his hand. "The things I do for friendship."

He dressed quickly, then held his hand out, which I gladly took. He pulled me closer for a pat on the back. "All right, I'll see you at the studio in a bit?"

"Yes. And remember, we're going to do a quick run-through of our set list, and then we're heading straight to the magazine offices for the interview and photo shoot, so pack up everything you need for the day." I paused, blinking in disbelief. I still couldn't believe the words *photo shoot* came out of my mouth. True, it wasn't anything fancy—just a quick shoot in the magazine's small studio. But everyone had to start somewhere. And this was the start of something big. I could feel it.

Luke swung his leg over the windowsill, straddling it as he studied where to land in the hedges below.

"Okay, bro. I'll catch you later." He nudged my side with his elbow, but the motion knocked him off balance. He lost purchase on his precarious perch and tumbled to the rosebushes below, hitting the mulch with a muffled thud.

My jaw dropped as I leaned out the window.

"Are you okay, dude?" I asked, and it came out more as a hiss than a whisper.

He scampered to his feet, brushing off the dirt from the front of his shirt. Correction—the front of *my* shirt.

"Ow," he mouthed, rubbing his back. His hands

flew to his face, pawing the surface to check for any scratches. We had a photo shoot this afternoon, and he definitely didn't want to look jacked up for that.

"I'll be all right, but—" He poked a finger through a hole in the shirtsleeve of my Rush T-shirt. "I'm sorry, man."

"Ugh this is the last time I loan you anything. Remember what happened to my LA Gears?"

"That wasn't my fault! Reggie spilled a slushie on them." He brought a fist up to his mouth, trying to cover his laugh. "Oh, come on. Don't be mad. You know you love me."

"I do. But I don't like you very much right now." I turned to look behind me. The floorboards in the hallway creaked again, and I knew my parents would overhear my conversation with Luke if we continued talking across the lawn. I turned my attention back to Luke, who had discovered another hole in the sleeve.

"Looks like that bush knows Morse code." He chuckled, making fake SOS beeping sounds.

"I'll see you at the studio later." I shooed him with my hands, hoping he'd disappear without any further noise. I seriously didn't want my parents to see Luke sneaking out. They might get the wrong idea. Or worse—they might take away my drumsticks.

Then I heard the front door squeak as it swung open, and tan slippers stepped over the threshold. My dad walked across the stoop, his mug of coffee steaming as he took a measured sip. My chest caved in—he was honestly the last person I wanted to see right now. His eyebrows furrowed as he looked wordlessly at Luke, who was in one of my shirts just outside my ground-floor window. It was clear he'd just snuck out of my room.

I could *feel* the blood drain from my face.

"Hi, Mr. Mercer." Luke waved sheepishly from the lawn, awkwardly putting a hand over his shoulder to hide his tattered sleeve.

Correction—*my* sleeve.

"Luke," my dad grumbled, barely loud enough for me to hear. "It's a bit early to be talking loudly on the lawn. I see you spent the night."

"Yes, sir."

"Dad, it seriously isn't what it looks like." I hung my head low, embarrassed to be having this conversation.

Not that my dad would ever take the time to know this, but I wasn't joking when I told Luke he wasn't my type. He was kinda messy, and I preferred someone a little cooler and quieter—like Luke Perry from *Beverly Hills, 90210.* Now *that* was my kind of guy.

And I wouldn't be sneaking the guy I liked out of a

window. I hoped one day I could bring someone home through the front door, and he would be welcomed with open arms just like my sister's college boyfriends were. But that didn't matter right now.

"I don't want to hear it." My dad held his hand up in my direction. "Whatever y'all do is . . . that's your business."

"Mr. Mercer, I just crashed for the night while I'm working out some stuff with my parents."

"They don't approve?" His ears perked up, as if he would find vindication in the fact that Luke's parents didn't approve of his *lifestyle*, either.

That's what they called it—a *lifestyle*—as if being gay was a choice I'd made.

My blood started to boil. And by the look on Luke's face, he was offended on my behalf. His lips parted as if he was about to say something, but I cut him off before he had a chance to mouth off.

"It's okay," I said, even though it was a lie. I nodded at him, trying to convince him to let it go. I checked my watch and cleared my throat. "You better get going if you wanna catch the eight o'clock bus."

"You sure?" He gritted his teeth, setting his jaw tight as he took one last look at my dad's imposing fig-ure on the stoop. When I nodded, he tramped across my sloped lawn toward the gate leading to the street, clearly peeved at our tense exchange.

"I meant what I said, Alex." My dad's finger shook as he pointed at me. "You do what you want but not under my roof. Understand?"

I mumbled an acknowledgment, then ducked back in the window, eager to put some distance between me and my dad's judgmental glare. I closed my eyes and breathed deeply.

Today is still going to be a great day.

I took an extra-long shower before hiding in my room until my laundry was finished, then dressed quickly—pink shirt and all! My duffel was filled to bursting when I left my bedroom. I had our band folder in it, which included our paperwork for the Orpheum and the interview sheets for the magazine later. I packed an extra pair of clothes, too, just in case I wanted to crash at the studio instead of coming home late again.

Who was I kidding? I *definitely* wanted to stay at the studio tonight. I could picture my friends' faces blushed and bright after crushing our showcase at the Orpheum. I could almost see the celebration we'd have in the studio later. That thought had me smiling when I walked into the living room.

"Well," I said with a sigh to the back of my dad's

head. He grunted in response. My mom looked away from the TV long enough to give me a tepid smile. "I'm going to the studio."

"Have fun, dear," Mom said, turning back to her show.

"Remember we have our showcase at the Orpheum tonight," I said in a low voice, unsure if they cared. But I swung my bag over my shoulder and set it on the ground. Rummaging through it, I pulled out two tickets from my folder. I heaved myself upward and set them on the coffee table. "I know you said you were busy tonight, but these are for you. In case you change your mind."

I wanted my parents to be interested in my life. I wanted them to see *me* and accept me with open arms. Music was in my soul—as much a part of me as my own two hands. But all they saw was my *lifestyle*.

My dad looked up, making brief eye contact with me before turning his gaze down to my pink shirt.

"That's what you're wearing?" he asked gruffly.

For a moment, my smile faltered, but then I straightened my back, squaring my shoulders proudly. I'd always liked the color pink. It was time I stopped hiding from myself and started living my own life—out of the shadow of my parents' expectations.

"I'm ready to rock and roll," I said with confidence as I scooped my bag off the floor. I grabbed the doorknob, resisting the urge to turn back and look at my parents. I wanted to move forward. And right now, that meant I was moving toward the studio, my drum set, and my band—my chosen family.

Julie

I stuck my head in my parents' room to find Tía with a towel wrapped around her head, wearing a pleasant change of wardrobe—a giant gray sweatshirt that I think belonged to my dad. She hunched over the Scrabble board between her and my mom, frowning at her letters while my mom slipped her feet into her bubbling foot spa.

"Okay, I'm heading over to Flynn's," I said, with a wave.

"Have fun, Angel Face," Mom said as she added more bath salts to her water. "Remember, you're baby-sitting Carlos tonight after dinner while your father and I go out. So don't disappear on me."

"Mamá." I looked at the time on my phone. "It's only two. I'll be back in *plenty* of time."

"Good, because your father's cooking tonight." She wiggled her eyebrows, then bit her lip to hide her smile.

"Ay, dios mío." Tía shook her head. "Good luck with *that*."

"Mom's been teaching him, so I'm sure it'll be at least okay-ish."

I waved goodbye and made a beeline for the stairs, smiling as I listened to their laughter fill the house. I grabbed my keys off the counter, excited to spend the afternoon with my bestie. Shortly after I'd texted Flynn, she'd answered back, saying I had to come over this afternoon. She had something she wanted to show me.

But before I made it out the door, I caught sight of my dad sitting hunched over a very large cookbook at the table. He looked above the rim of the book, his eyebrows knitting together.

"Do you think homemade pasta tastes better than store-bought pasta?"

"I think all carbs are created equally delicious. Why?" I eyed the book title suspiciously: *The Italian Chef's Master Class*. That didn't sound like anything my dad should be reading. He was more of a beginner in the kitchen. "Are you thinking about making your own noodles tonight?"

"It says right here in the book that fresh pasta will

soak up the flavor, making every bite taste *delizioso*." He frowned at the page, scratching his graying hair. "But it also says you need a standing mixer with this weird-looking attachment thingy. Do you know if we have anything like this?"

He lifted the book, struggling with the hefty weight as he held it up to my face. My eyes crossed as I looked at the list of instructions and at the diagram of the attachment.

"Um." I bit my lip, trying to figure out the most diplomatic way to say this. "Have you talked to mom about this?"

"I didn't want to disturb her spa day," he said with a shrug, rubbing the back of his neck. "Your mom deserves a little downtime—she's been so tired lately. And it's date night, you know. I want to make it special."

I hugged him, squeezing him tight. When he wrapped both his arms around me, I closed the book over his shoulder. He whipped his head around.

"Hey!"

"Remember, we'll love anything you cook tonight— even regular noodles, okay?" I backed away slowly, making sure he understood that he should *definitely not* complicate his cooking duties tonight. But as I opened the door, I swear I saw him crack open the cookbook again. I wondered if I'd come home to a plume of flour and gnarly-looking linguine later.

Once outside, I checked the time on my phone and was distracted by an Instagram notification for Nick. I leaned on one of the front porch's columns, my thumb hovering over his profile picture. I was prepared to dive in, but I was startled by a loud bang.

"BOO!" Carlos shouted, stomping his foot again.

"AHHH!" I screamed, losing my grip on my phone. I fumbled it in the air, my fingers desperately trying to catch it, but it bounced off—straight into the bushes. "Carlos!"

"Gotcha." He pumped his fist in the air, his smug smile growing wider.

Lately, my little brother was super fixated on his two favorite things—his new baseball team and jumping out of corners and scaring the living daylights out of everyone in the house. You'd think I'd wise up to his game and wouldn't be scared of the scream anymore, but it got me *every time*.

Seriously. Every freakin' time!

"Oh, I'll get you back. When you least expect it," I grumbled as I hopped down the steps, making my way into the landscaped bushes that lined the porch stairs.

My long curls snagged on the branches, tugging at my scalp as I pawed the ground for my phone.

Oh, I'm going to get him back good.

"You'll never catch a pro at his own game." And with that, he shut the front door behind him, a devilish grin on his face. I pitied my dad and his cookbook. They were likely his next scare victims.

Brushing the dirt off my phone, I started the eight-minute journey to Flynn's house. I eyed my neighbor's house across the street. If I cut through Mr. Canneli's yard, I'd shave the time in half, but he didn't take kindly to trespassers.

Trust me, I'd tried.

I knocked softly on Flynn's front door, then turned the handle, letting myself inside. The Taylor house was my second home, after all. I didn't need to knock. I shimmied past an overgrown fern in the entryway, thriving in the bright room. Flynn's house had so many windows, and her parents filled every frame with plants. Succulents dangled from pots that hung above the window while ferns and spider plants fought for space on various tables scattered around the house.

I took a deep breath. You could almost feel the extra oxygen.

Flynn zoomed onto the second-floor landing, disturbing a hanging plant dangling from the banister.

I think that one is new.

"Hey, weirdo." She waved her hand, telling me to get upstairs pronto.

"What up, cray cray."

When I joined her at the top, she pulled me in for a tight hug. "Okay, I have good news and I have *great* news. Which one do you want first?"

"Uh." I bit the inside of my tongue, thinking about it. "The good news."

"I thought you'd *never* ask." She grabbed my arm, then tugged me into her room, a decidedly *different* space than the lush greenery of the rest of the house. Flynn's room was an *explosion* of color. Pinks, blues, metallics, glitter, and neons assaulted you as soon as you walked in.

It was one of the many things I loved about Flynn. When we were six, Flynn almost cried over an assignment about our favorite color because she didn't want to choose.

"The good news is that I have perfected our debut Double Trouble song." She kicked her leg in the air as if she couldn't contain her joy.

I approached with caution, as I did with all things Double Trouble—the band we'd been saying we were going to form since the dawn of time. Between home-work and auditioning for the Los Feliz Performing Arts music program and now my latest drama with Carrie, our band plans had fallen to the wayside. But every now and then, Flynn could always be trusted to revive the fantasy.

"Okay, stand here." She gripped my shoulders and scooted me to the edge of her room. She looked me squarely in the face, a glint of mischief in her eyes. "You're going to drool when you hear this. It could be Double Trouble's first hit!"

I grinned, intrigued. Flynn was a talented lyricist, so whatever she had cooked up for the band's first song was going to be music gold.

But the name! Seriously, we could *not* settle for Double Trouble. We were going to have to come up with something better before we actually made a real attempt at performing.

"Are we still opposed to Gruesome Twosome?" I asked, raising my eyebrow and laughing.

"Just watch!" She slid on a pair of retro shades from her back pocket as she walked to the makeshift DJ booth on her desk. She slipped on the sunglasses, switched on her old-school keyboard, and pressed play on her laptop. Familiar opening chords filled the room.

She raised her hands in the air, wiggling her fingers as she brought them down slowly. Pointing her toe to the ground, she bobbed her hips to the beat, her silver bike shorts shimmering. I had to hand it to her—Flynn knew how to drum up drama.

"I *can't* with 'Final Countdown' right now," I said, trying not to laugh through her routine.

"It's a total classic." She held her hand up as the music reached a crescendo. She rounded the corner of her desk, her fingers poised over her electric piano. "Here we go. REMIX!"

Get ready for this throwback
This duo don't know how to act
In this final countdown
Don't wanna be a letdown
Think it's time to wipe that frown up
off your face

"Oh, snap!" I shouted, jumping over to meet Flynn by her desk. I was always down for an impromptu dance party. In fact, we broke out in random dances almost every day. Spurred on by my excitement, Flynn returned her fingers to the piano keys and rolled into her next verse.

Join me in these streets, yo
While I play piano
Show me your joy
Come on and make some noise!

I looked at the DJ program running on her desktop—all the sound bars were running wild as the remix played on. She'd worked hard on this rap, and that wasn't all she'd been practicing. Her skills on the piano had also caught my attention.

"Flynn! You're playing the *piano*," I said, my jaw hanging wide open. I pointed to the keyboard, where she'd competently lumbered through the notes.

"Girl, *please*. I was hoping you'd take the keys."

"But you've been practicing, and you're getting kinda good. Well, better anyway." Admittedly, piano playing wasn't Flynn's strong suit. Rapping was where she really shined. She could turn a phrase at the snap of her fingers, but really all types of music had a place in her heart. In some ways, she reminded me of my mom in her ability to pick up any instrument and figure it out.

I wished I could do that. My piano and singing audition had gotten me into one of the most competitive music programs on the West Coast. But sometimes

I felt like I was still discovering the piano, even though I had been playing since I was four years old.

"I'll never catch up to your skills, though." Flynn lowered the volume on her computer and leaned on the edge of her desk.

"Maybe we could get some straps on that keyboard, so that you can play standing up." I was being facetious, but Flynn obviously didn't see it that way. She gasped.

"Now you're talking. A keytar! The eighties and nineties are making a comeback. It'll be the *best*. What do you think?"

"I think it sounds awesome." I plopped down on the edge of her bed with a sigh. "But can we work on the name?"

"The Dynamic Duo?" Her hands flew above her head. "Ooooh! The Witchy Sissies?"

"We'll keep brainstorming," I said, deadpan.

"Look, I know it still needs some work, but the point is: It's the countdown to starting our throwback-musical-girl-gang band. One, two, three—you and me. What do you say?"

I squinted, thinking about her countdown, and then my gaze grew distant, blurring as I thought about the untitled song Mom and I were working on. Just like my mom, who stopped everything the moment lyrics grabbed her attention, I needed to find a pen. I darted across the room, sliding Flynn's desk drawer open in search of something to write with.

"Uh, can I help you?" She knelt down so that I could see the confusion on her face.

"Do you have paper?" I asked, gripping a purple gel pen in my hands. "I think I just found a piece of a song, and it's all thanks to you!"

Ugh, why didn't I bring my notebook?

I could have kicked myself for leaving my freewriting journal in my room. It was where I wrote all my ideas—my daydreams and tiny musings, basically whatever came into my head. Everything was an ingredient for a song. I just didn't expect a eureka moment so soon after my writing session with Mom.

"Ahh! I *love* it when genius strikes." Flynn slid a notepad off her bookshelf and handed it to me. "Hurry, write it down."

The words poured out of me and onto the page. I eyed the paper, envisioning where it fit in the song. Smiling, I looked up at Flynn. "I think I just found the pre-chorus."

She leaned over my shoulder, pursing her lips as she looked at my scribbles.

And it's one, two, three, four times
That I'll try for one more night
Light a fire in my eyes
I'm going out of my mind

"The first verse is about how everything moves so fast when you're chasing your dreams. And how you've got to keep pushing and never look back." I smiled, thinking about singing it with my mom this morning.

"That sounds *ahh*-mazing." She snapped her fingers, her orange nail polish glinting in the sunlight. "Can't wait to hear the rest of it."

"You will soon. It's almost finished." I searched my brain, just in case the song's chorus was hiding somewhere up there. I shook my head—it wasn't ready to hop on the page yet. "Sorry, I kinda blew up your surprise."

"No worries." Flynn twiddled her fingers in front of her face. "But now it's time for that great news, huh?"

7

Julie

Flynn skipped over to the bed and sat next to me, practically vibrating with energy. If her elaborate Double Trouble rap routine was only the *good* surprise, I could only imagine what her *great* surprise was.

"So, I went shopping this morning at my mom's store." She flipped her long braids over her shoulder, showing off a new pair of earrings — neon-yellow lightning bolts.

"I hope you realize how lucky you are." I sighed, looking around Flynn's room. Not that she needed more stuff. Seriously, this place was packed to the brim with clothes and accessories. But when your mom owns one of the funkiest boutiques on Melrose Avenue, the premiere clothier to the eclectic customer, it's basically your God-given right to shop.

"Well, you're about to luck out, too, because I saw the most *fire* dress that had Julie Molina's quinceañera written *all* over it." She clasped her hands together and brought the bundle of fingers to her face. "It came in on consignment, and I just couldn't let my mom put it on display—not before you had a chance to take a look at it."

"It's not a poufy pink dress, right?" I asked, scrunching my face up. There was nothing wrong with the color pink, but I wanted to do something different with my outfit—wear something off the beaten path. "I don't want to look like a cupcake."

"Girl, *bye*." She waved dismissively. "I know your taste like the back of my hand."

"That's true." I looked around the room, searching for a mound of tulle hiding behind one of Flynn's garment racks. "Can I see it?"

"I thought you'd *never* ask." She sprang from the bed and opened her bedroom door. Leaning out she yelled into the hallway, "Mom, we're ready! Bring it up, pretty please with a cherry on top."

"Okay," I heard Misha's voice reply from somewhere deep in the house. The stairs creaked as she made her way to the second floor.

All of a sudden, my heart rate fluttered and my pulse quickened. Every time I tried on a dress, I hoped it would be the right one, but it never was. The dresses were always missing that extra edge, that special something that made it as unique as I was. Could Flynn and her mom really have found *the one*? Anticipation and a little apprehension flooded my veins. I grabbed Flynn's hand, bouncing on the balls of my feet. She squeezed my fingers, her smile growing wider.

"Thanks for this. Carrie and I were supposed to hit up a couple dress shops this weekend, but then she—"

"Flaked!" Flynn interjected, pursing her lips. She wasn't the biggest fan of Carrie's, and it showed every time I mentioned her name. And with the way Carrie had been treating me lately, maybe Flynn was onto something. "You'll forget all about her mean-girl ways once you lay your eyes on this dress."

"Knock, knock," said a singsongy voice from the other side of the door. Flynn's mom shoved it open with a tap of her foot, tan moccasins with beaded fringe— the queen of eclectic fashion. "There's my second child."

In one hand she lugged an *enormous* white garment bag, which must have been the mystery dress, and in the other hand she had a plate of snacks with foil over the top.

"Hi, Misha," I said with a wave. It always felt weird calling an adult by their first name, but Flynn's parents didn't like formalities or titles. *Call me Misha for goodness' sake,* she used to say, and it stuck. I grabbed the plate from her and set it on Flynn's nightstand. As soon as I did, Misha scooped me up in her arms.

"Uh! This is so exciting. You girls are becoming women." She clutched her chest, her shoulder-length dreads grazing the straps of her green tie-dyed dress. Misha wore a *lot* of tie-dye—not in rainbow colors. That wasn't her color palette—or at least that's what she'd told me *several* times. She was of the earth and wore her trusted greens and browns mostly.

Yeah, Flynn's parents were kinda *out there*.

She set the garment bag on the edge of the bed and started unzipping it slowly. Her grin widened as she parted the fabric, revealing a truly *amazing* two-piece dress. My hand flew over my mouth, and I gasped.

"Do you like it?" Misha raised both of her eyebrows, nodding expectantly.

"Like it? I *love* it." I ran my fingers along the top part of the dress—a bustier bedazzled in white pearls and black sequins. The bottom half consisted of a beautiful cascading tulle skirt—not too poufy, with layers upon layers of purple and gold. Unlike Flynn, I did have a favorite color, and it was purple. I imagined myself in this dress, and thought I might look like a dahlia, my mom's favorite flower, which was quickly becoming my favorite, too. "It's *perfect*."

"Told ya." Flynn nodded proudly. "It gives off major Selena vibes."

"Oh my gosh, you're totally right." I gripped my chest, seeing Selena written all over the bustier. She was one of my all-time faves. Only Trevor Wilson competed with her for the top spot in my heart.

Flynn was at the top of that list, too.

My best friend was incredible. I threw my arm around her shoulders, feeling immensely lucky to have her in my corner—especially in light of Carrie's current cold shoulder treatment. My heart blazed with pride, and I squeezed Flynn tighter.

"You were right." I wiped a teary eye with the back of my hand. "The nineties are *totally* making a comeback."

Flynn shimmied out of my arms and her nostrils flared. She frowned and looked over her shoulder.

"Wait." She sniffed the air again, her gaze zeroing in on the plate of snacks I'd set on her nightstand. Flynn raised a skeptical eyebrow, her nostrils still wiggling. "What's under that foil?"

Luke

I was still ticked off by the time I got off the bus in Los Feliz. I waved to the driver as he closed the door, then watched the bus lumber down the street. I worried about Alex sometimes. He was one of the brightest lights I'd seen, and I didn't want his parents' judgmental weirdness to snuff that out.

One of these days, I'm going to give his dad a piece of my mind.

Thinking about Alex's family got me thinking about my own, and about the dysfunction that had ripped us apart. I hoped that didn't happen to Alex, too.

The walk to the studio was uphill, through the winding roads of Los Feliz. It was a workout, which kinda sucked—I was still dog-tired from our late-night concert. But getting my blood pumping woke me up a bit.

My keys rattled against the studio door as I unlocked it for the day. I loved this time of the morning, when the light was dim, fresh with the promise of emerging brightness. The sun bounced off the vaulted beams, bringing the converted garage alive. The whole space was painted in a soft gray, probably to make the ceiling look higher than it was. It sure was bigger than any part of my squat house with low ceilings.

That still didn't keep me from missing home.

I opened the door to the bathroom in the back corner, pulling the dangling chain to turn on the lights. The fluorescent bulb flickered to life, providing a dim sphere of light in the otherwise dank confines of the narrow room. Turning the knob on the shower, I held my fingers under the water, waiting for it to warm up enough to jump in. After a few minutes it warmed *slightly*, and from my experience, this was as good as it would get. I pulled Alex's borrowed shirt over my head, steeling myself for yet another cold shower, then stepped in.

After my quick rinse off, I dried my hair with a towel and strolled across the studio, kicking an empty can of soda underneath the weathered couch—my current bed, or *nest* as Reggie called it. I plopped down, debating whether or not I should nap until the boys came for practice.

But that chilly shower had woken me up, and I was feeling the pull of my music.

These quiet hours were usually when my writing flourished. I unlatched my acoustic guitar case, taking a moment to run my fingers over the polished wood before taking my guitar out. I opened my notebook—I wanted to play around with some new lyrics, but the pages flipped to an older song.

"Unsaid Emily."

It was the song I'd written for my mom. I'm not sure why I wrote it—it's not like she would ever hear it. She and I hadn't talked in months—not since I left home last winter. I ran my fingers over my messy chicken scratch, across the turmoil waging war on the page. I'd opened my notebook to this song so many times, it had a permanent crease in the binding to *this* spread. Scribbles in the margins and tons of scratch outs littered the page. And they all boiled down to one thing:

How can I talk to my mom again?

I still didn't know the answer to that question.

Maybe that's why I didn't know what to do about Alex's situation—because I still hadn't figured out how to deal with my own estrangement. I wasn't sure where to even begin. There was so much hurt between me and my mom—such a feeling of betrayal. I closed my eyes, remembering the last time we spoke. We'd said some awful things to each other.

She'd slammed her hands on the kitchen table and shoved out her chair, her cheeks heating with a burning blush. She was angry with me about missing school to take an extra shift at the diner. I'd reasoned that I'd needed the money to buy a new guitar—it wasn't like *she* would give me the money. She never believed in my passion. She never thought it would go anywhere.

Or at least that's what I'd thought.

My mom had stormed into the living room, exasperated. *That's it*, she'd said. *You're grounded*. And then she stormed off to my room to grab my guitar.

I lost it. I'm not proud of my behavior. I still cringe when I remember the words I said, *I hate you!* Tears burned my eyes as I hastily packed a bag. And I remember thinking: *What are you doing?* I'd had a whole speech planned, something that might bring her to my way of thinking. Something that might bring us closer together. But all that was thrown out the window in a moment of hot, flared tempers. That regret was written all over the page.

> First things first
> We start the scene in reverse
> All of the lines rehearsed
> Disappeared from my mind

I truly meant what I wrote. If I could rewind time to go back to the exact moment of our breakdown, I would. I'd find another way to ask my mom to give me a chance—to let me try to make a career out of music. Was there room for forgiveness? I got out my guitar and strummed the notes that corresponded with the words, singing the words under my breath.

> When things got loud
> One of us running out
> I should have turned around
> But I had too much pride

> No time
> For goodbyes
> Didn't get to apologize
> Pieces of a clock that lies broken

If I could take us back
If I could just do that
And write in every empty space
The words "I love you" in replace
Then maybe time would not erase me

If you could only know
I never let you go
And the words I most regret
Are the ones I never meant to leave
Unsaid Emily

My voice hitched, and I paused my playing. At the same time, the barn door to the studio swung open, catching me unaware. Bobby walked in, lugging his guitar case onto the side table, crushing the fast-food wrappers littered there in the process.

Okay, maybe I need to do some cleaning.

His eyebrows quirked up when he saw me sitting on the couch, hunched over my guitar.

"You okay, dude?" he asked, crossing the room in a few short strides.

"I'm fine." I ran my fingers through my damp hair, turning away from him so that he couldn't see the lie in my eyes. Bobby and I had been friends since we were kids—long before I'd met Alex and Reggie. He knew when something was eating away at me.

And he knew it now.

"Was that the song I think it was?" He slid my notebook across the coffee table and scanned the page, then plopped down on the couch with a heavy sigh. "You wanna add it to the set list for tonight?"

"I don't know if I want to let the whole crowd in on my mom issues." I shrugged with a strained laugh. "I've just been thinking about her a lot lately. You know, I thought about inviting her to the show tonight, but . . ." I sighed, looking out the window. "I don't think she'll ever talk to me again."

"She's your *mom*." He leaned forward, his lips pursed. "Give her a chance."

"You think?" I sputtered another sigh. I didn't realize I'd been holding my breath until I finally deeply exhaled. I picked up an empty fast-food container from the table and left the couch in search of the trash can, suddenly eager for a distraction.

"I'll help you clean." Bobby got up and started picking up discarded napkins and Coke cans.

He always knew how to help, even when I didn't ask him for it.

Reggie

The chords of my bass strings reverberated off the walls of our studio as I sang the last line of "Now or Never," my personal favorite of our entire set list. It captured the energy of this moment in our lives—the moment when everything was on the verge of changing for the better. That's why it was going to be the finale of our showcase.

The ladies were gonna *love it*—especially since I'd be wearing this seriously cool vintage leather jacket I'd recently picked up at a thrift store in Santa Monica. It had a sweet chain that wrapped underneath my pits and horizontal zipper compartments across each side, one of which could easily hold a bottle of minty mouthwash spray.

Hello, ladies.

But while I had opted for more clothing, Luke

had gone for less—he'd chopped off the sleeves of his T-shirt.

"At this point, you should just go shirtless." I chuckled as I pointed to his plunging sleeve holes. "Will you be doing this to all your shirts?"

"It's actually *my* shirt. Long story." Alex shook his head, holding a hand up. I kept my mouth shut, even though I was burning to ask if it had anything to do with his pink-tinted Fresh shirt. Alex turned to Luke, his lip jutted out in a pout. "Did you really have to rip them all the way off, man?"

"Alex, come on. The sleeves were toast." Luke held his arms up and shrugged.

"Will you be taking some of the bottom off, too, and turning it into a crop top?" I asked, jokingly. But my chuckles faded—at this point I wouldn't put it past him.

"*Ha-ha.* I've only done this to two shirts, and I had reasons for both." He punched me playfully on the arm. Then he tilted his head, as if he just remembered something important. He turned to face our rhythmic guitarist. "Bobby, can I talk to you for a sec?"

"Sure." He nodded and followed Luke over to the table on the other side of the studio. Luke clearly wanted to put some distance between us while he gave

Bobby some notes on his performance. This was not the first time he'd needed to tighten his sound—and who better to tweak his chord progressions than our lead guitarist?

"You're still coming in a tad too early on the last chorus," Luke said in a low voice, trying not to be too loud. But the acoustics in the studio were incredible, and Alex and I could hear every word. "Just pause for a second longer before jumping into *rising up right now*. Got it?"

"I gotcha," Bobby mumbled, fingering the chords on his guitar. He hung his head low, a look of determination on his face. I really felt for the guy. Playing guitar didn't come as easily for Bobby as it did for Luke. His expression kinda reminded me of my little brother. Steve was always begging me to teach him to play bass. (What better way to escape the house for a bit, especially when Mom and Dad were in the middle of one of their epic arguments?) But his fingers couldn't quite keep up with his enthusiasm. He sometimes got ahead of himself and fumbled the notes, but I couldn't ever fault him for his excitement. I felt the same way about Bobby. Sometimes his passion just got in the way.

So, patience was the name of the game.

That being said, I *really* hoped Bobby would tighten up his timing on the last part of the song. It was our finale, and I really wanted us to end with a bang.

"Cool," Luke said, patting him on the back before waving us over to where they were standing. We walked over to the table in the center of the room, which was surprisingly bare. Luke had obviously done some cleaning. He snaked his arm around my shoulders and gripped it tightly, practically vibrating with excitement. "I think we're ready, boys."

His voice echoed off the rafters of the converted garage, and I felt the *life* that always reverberated off the studio's walls—we all felt it. This place had *soul*.

In many ways the studio was like a life raft. It had seen us through the shaky storms of high school and thousands of rehearsals. It was a place where Alex knew he could always be himself without judgment, and somewhere I could find quiet and calm when things at home were loud and tense. And now that Luke didn't have a home to go to, this studio had become our refuge.

"Not to sound cheesy or anything, but I love this place." I took a deep breath, exhaling as I tilted my head toward the rafters. "It gave us the space to grow, you know?"

"I know what you mean. And that gives me an idea." Luke ran to the mini fridge that sat next to the bathroom.

"*Uh-oh.*" I smirked. "Does it involve all of us ripping our T-shirts up, because I might have to take a rain check." I gripped my leather jacket and pulled it tighter, hiding my crisp white shirt.

"Yeah, the burger shack on Sunset has a NO SHIRT, NO SHOES, NO SERVICE sign out front." Alex chortled, mumbling something about the Hamburglar under his breath. "Reggie will have his burgers."

"Guys, guys." Luke returned to the group, his arms full of soda cans. "Let's make a toast—no, a *pact*—with the studio. Whatever happens tonight, let's always remember this place."

I sighed, giving the old place another once-over. From the dusty windows to the faded rug, and even the overgrown ivy and untrimmed bushes in the backyard. This was home. It felt right to show the place some gratitude.

"I don't know for sure whether we'll sign with a label tonight"—Luke inhaled sharply, like his heart rate was skyrocketing at the mere mention of it—"but I know this place is special. Something magical happens when we play here, and we bring that to the stage. So let's toast to the studio."

"Hear, hear!" I raised my soda in the air. "To the studio!"

"The studio!" Alex joined me in raising his can.

"Our studio!" said Bobby, following suit.

"May we always have a seat at this table." Luke touched his can to ours, pausing for a moment to let the toast sink in. Then we brought the cans to our lips and chugged a couple sips. Luke burped just as Alex clapped his hands, snapping my attention in his direction.

"I've got our backstage passes." He held up a green folder, filled with all the band's business.

"And I brought my mom's old van. Gassed her up this morning," Bobby said proudly.

"Anyone remember to bring pens?" Alex asked.

"Got 'em right here." I dug in my back pocket and pulled out an assortment of colored pens—a dozen of them in every color of the rainbow. "Extra colors for the *ladies*. And I didn't want to jinx it, but I bought this really cool metallic one. You know, platinum status."

"Nice," Luke said hungrily, his eyes growing wider as he likely thought of Sunset Curve reaching the big leagues. I had to admit, I was thinking the same thing. The idea of Sunset Curve making it big—the fans, the tours, and Steve in the front row, watching his awesome big brother rock out for a sold-out crowd—it was all so close.

"I think that covers it." Luke sighed in satisfaction, taking one last look around our sacred space. A frown crept across his face. "Something tells me we're forgetting something."

"Uh, *hello*." Alex brandished the band folder above his head. "I run a tight ship over here."

"Cool, cool," Luke said, unwilling to argue with our task master.

"Who wants to help me stuff my drum set into the back of Bobby's car?" Alex asked. It wasn't really a question. We all had to help. We weren't famous enough to have roadies to load and unload our gear, so whenever we did a show, we had to stuff all the studio into the back of Bobby's hand-me-down van.

It could take hours to dismantle and set up the whole thing again. That's why we had to pack everything up so early. We'd need to head straight from the *Spin* magazine interview to the Orpheum for our six o'clock sound check. And then curtain call was at nine.

There was barely any wiggle room. Hence Alex's folder of organization.

"Let's load the strings first." I flung my bass strap

over my shoulder and followed my bandmates out the door. Next time we saw this place, we'd be well on our way to stardom. I broke out into a toothy grin and practically skipped to the van with visions of platinum status dancing in my head.

Flynn

My nostrils flared as I sniffed the smelly mystery plate my mom had brought into my room. When she saw my horrified look, she turned her attention from Julie's quinceañera dress to me, blinking away the dew in her eyes. I hated to break up the moment—I was just as excited as they were about the Selena dress—but I couldn't think straight with the cloud of stink floating in the air.

"It's tofu." My mom shook her head as if the contents of the foil-covered plate were self-evident. "One of your favorites."

"That doesn't smell like any tofu I've ever eaten." I frowned, looking to Julie for support, but her attention was still on the dress. She gazed dreamily at it, oblivious to my conversation.

Geez, if she can ignore this nasty tofu, she must be in love *with the dress!*

"It's tofu with a twist." My mom unveiled the plate to reveal a pile of brownish cubes and leaned forward to enjoy the bouquet. Less-than-subtle notes of boiled eggs and sweaty feet were unleashed onto the room. Julie snapped out of her dream dress reverie.

"Oh." Julie brought a fist up to her mouth, trying to hide her gag.

"It's slightly fermented tofu. Your father and I used to eat it all the time when we were in China. You can only find the authentic stuff downtown."

I laughed nervously, trying not to breathe.

"Don't worry, it's not going to get you woozy. It's not *that* fermented," she said, throwing her head back and letting out a tinkling laugh.

It's already *making me woozy.*

I stepped farther away from the plate, grabbing Julie's arm and dragging us to fresher air. We stood next to a window on the far side of my bedroom. I pushed it open even more, praying for maximum air circulation—I'd take hurricane-force winds!

Look, I'm no stranger to eating foods off the beaten path. When I was a baby, I ate a full vegetarian diet. When I was in kindergarten, I was the only kid who brought sushi to school. In a lot of ways, I was grateful for my parents' adventurous taste buds and even more grateful for my dad's endless pursuit of sustainable food production. It made me a better global citizen, and I liked that.

But sometimes they missed the mark. By the smell of that tofu, Mom had *really* missed the mark on this one.

"I thought you girls would want a snack." Mom popped a piece in her mouth, nodding with a close-mouthed smile like it was the most delicious thing she'd ever eaten.

"Oh, thanks, Misha." Julie coughed, trying to not gag again. She looked at me, her eyes tight as she searched my face for help.

"Mom, thanks, but I think we were just finishing up here."

"Come on, my young women. Broaden your horizons. Tear down the yolk of Western dietary limitations." She raised her eyebrows at me expectantly—she expected more from my taste buds. Then she grinned, leaning closer to me, whispering conspiratorially, "This is nothing. You should see the tofu that's kinda *hairy*."

Julie inhaled sharply, holding her breath as my mom lifted the plate closer to her nostrils.

"If you gals are planning on hanging out up here for

a while, you're welcome to stay for dinner, Julie." She shimmied her hips, dancing along to her menu plans. "Meat loaf, sound good?"

My mouth dropped.

Did I hear that right?

We weren't technically vegetarians here. My dad worked for a sustainable seafood distributor that sourced ethically raised aquaponic foodstuffs, so we ate a lot of fish, especially when his company had a surplus. He was super concerned about sustainability, so beef and pork weren't commonly featured at our dinner table. That's why when I heard the words *meat loaf* come out of Mom's mouth, I was instantly intrigued.

"What's the catch?" I asked, raising my eyebrows. This house hadn't seen red meat in years—*literally*.

"Don't worry." My mom covered her mouth as she munched on another piece of fermented tofu. "It's a vegan quinoa meatless loaf."

Yeesh. Hard pass.

I bit the inside of my cheek and tried not to flare my nostrils as I looked over at Julie, who was smiling nervously at my mom. As soon as Mom dove for another slice of tofu, our gazes met. I shook my head vigorously, warning her not to come anywhere near the meat loaf.

"Misha, I honestly can't thank you enough for the

dress." Julie nodded toward the Selena dress laying on the bed. I found myself wondering if the tofu smell would stick to the fibers. I'd have to offer to dry-clean it.

"Yeah, thanks, Mom. But I think Julie has to get going." I gave the clock an exaggerated look. "She's, uh, helping cook dinner later."

"That's right." Julie nodded slowly, her smile widening. She was up to something. "*We* are helping my dad perfect his homemade pasta recipe."

Hallelujah, I'm saved. That's my girl!

Jules was saving me from a night of dietary horrors. This was one of the many reasons she was my best friend.

"So I'll have to try your new recipe later." I jutted my lip in a fake pout, hoping I wasn't hurting my mom's feelings too much. I loved her to freakin' pieces . . . just not her taste in food.

"Are you sure I can't interest you in a piece before you go?" My mom held the plate up to Julie.

"Ehh . . ." Julie cringed.

And that's when I decided to fall on my sword. I reached out to Mom's plate of fermented bean curd and plucked a piece from the top. "I'll try one."

My eyes began to water the closer I brought the tofu to my face, as if the smell was making me involuntarily cry. Julie's hands flew over her mouth, and her shoulders shook like she was laughing and gagging at the same time. My eyes tightened as I brought the cube to my lips.

I'm takin' one for the team, girl.

I popped it into my mouth, chewed quickly, and swallowed it nearly whole. It was penance for skipping out on dinner and an expression of gratitude for Jules, since she'd saved me from a horrendous meatless loaf.

I was squared up with the universe and karma and Black Jesus. I had earned the right to eat the Molinas' pasta dinner tonight. But right now I needed to wash this taste from my mouth. I smacked my lips, looking for a glass of water. As if she could read my mind, Julie handed me the one from my nightstand with a wink.

"Thanks," she whispered. "I'll see you in a couple hours?"

"Try and stop me," I said between gulps of water.

Nothing would keep me from spending time with my best friend.

11

Luke

The seating arrangements in the van were always the same, without fail. Alex liked to be in the back seat so he could look after his drum set, and Reggie liked to sit next to Alex so he could bug him. That left me riding up front while Bobby drove. I spent most of the ride hunched over my notebook, trying to come up with lyrics for a new ballad that I'd been kicking around.

I ripped out another page and crumpled it up. Nothing seemed like the right angle. Sometimes I wish I had a writing partner to bounce ideas off of—to make me better. I loved my boys, but they didn't really inspire any love songs.

Out of the corner of my eye, I could feel Bobby's gaze boring into me. I gave him a sidelong glance, and he quickly looked back at the road. I leaned closer to the window, hunching over my pages so that he couldn't sneak another peek at my work in progress.

All of a sudden, Bobby made a sharp turn across an intersection, drawing my attention to the road for the first time in miles. We were in a residential neighborhood with sprawling sloped lawns, manicured with pride. It slowly dawned on me that this wasn't just any neighborhood—it was *mine*.

"Dude." I gripped the armrests, my mouth agape. "What are we doing here?"

"Come on, Luke. We talked about this." Bobby looked over at me. "It's time to tell your mom how you feel."

"That's not your decision to make," I said, my voice rising several octaves. I folded my arms and looked out the window. "Turn around."

"Luke—"

"Turn around!" I said louder, drowning him out.

"I'm sorry, are we not on our way to the magazine shoot?" The faux leather seats squeaked as Alex shifted in the back. He scooted forward, peering out the windshield at the tree-lined residential streets whizzing by. He moaned, probably because Bobby had veered from his thorough directions—and our tight schedule. "Where are we?"

"I'll tell you where we are." I pointed to the stop sign in front of us. "We're right down the street from my parents' house, because Bobby can't mind his own business."

It came out harsher than I'd meant it to. Bobby was my oldest friend, and I didn't want to hurt his feelings. He got enough of that at home with his macho brothers. Maybe it was because we'd known each other for so long that he thought he could push me to run back home. But he'd miscalculated.

This was a *betrayal*.

"Oh, geez," Alex moaned. As if he could feel the temperature rising in the car, he slid back to his seat and rolled down his window.

"I mean, now that we're here, you might as well talk to her." Reggie leaned over the center console, gripping my headrest.

"I just don't think it's the right time," I said through gritted teeth.

"It's nobody's call but Luke's. You can't just *make* someone be cool with their parents." Alex folded his arms, scowling to himself as he stared out the window. I got the sense that he wasn't just talking about my situation—he was also talking about his wobbly relationship with his own folks. To my surprise, Reggie also caught his drift.

"Sorta get where your head's at, man." Reggie gripped Alex's shoulder, nodding with understanding.

The brakes squeaked to a halt as Bobby pulled in front of a familiar redbrick house. The cactus near the front door looked the same, albeit a bit bigger. And the large front windows were open like they always were. In fact, everything looked the same. It was as if I'd never left home.

Had they missed me? Had they even noticed I'd been gone?

My mom's ancient station wagon sat idle in the driveway, and it elicited the same reaction it always did. A surge of adrenaline shot through my veins—I was obviously nervous about the possibility of seeing her again. I slouched in my seat, sliding down so that my forehead barely cleared the bottom of the window.

"Look, you can be mad at me all you want," Bobby said, unlocking the doors. The locks sprang up at attention. "But your mom is inside right now. And you should give her this."

He set an envelope on the center console. The corners looked worn and there was a crease down the middle of it, like he'd been carrying it around for a while. I recognized it immediately—these were the tickets we were supposed to give our friends and family.

"They couldn't come?" I asked, my eyebrows knitting together.

"I didn't even bother asking." He shook his head with a huff. "My mom is on the road to support my brother at his football game. She wouldn't miss *that* for our show."

"I mean," Reggie said, scooting forward, "if you don't wanna talk to her, you could just leave the tickets at the door."

"Or leave a note?" Alex offered.

"I guess," I said, wondering what I would say. It would take ages to condense "Unsaid Emily" into a letter, and we didn't have the time for that. I could always keep it short and simple: *I love you. Talk soon?* But that left the door open for her to say she didn't want to see me.

That's what she'd said the last time I'd seen her—that she couldn't even look at me.

I eyed the front door, my eyes narrowing. I'd vowed never to come back here. I thought I was done with this place—*forever.* But even from the other side of the street, I could feel its pull. It was the gravity that home had on me.

And yet, there was still a nugget of uncertainty in my chest.

Before I could come to a decision, Bobby snatched the tickets off the center console and grabbed his door handle.

"If you're not gonna give her the tickets, then I will."

Alex

The van shuddered as Bobby slammed his door. With a nervous glance back at us, he walked toward the Pattersons' house. Luke scrambled over the gearshift to the driver's side of the car and cranked the window down as fast as he could.

"Get back here!" Luke hissed at Bobby's retreating figure. But he couldn't hear him. He was already across the street. "Bobby! So help me . . ."

Luke opened the door and tumbled out headfirst. Hopping up from the asphalt, he wiped his hands on the bottom of his shirt. Correction—*my* shirt. His arms pumped at his sides as he marched after Bobby.

Reggie leaned against the window, his nose pressing against the glass. He exhaled sharply, making the glass fog up. He wiped away the haze just in time to catch Bobby breaking into a jog to avoid being caught. Luke matched his pace, his arms outstretched as if he was ready to tackle him.

"You think this will end well?" he asked, turning to look over his shoulder at me.

"I don't know, man." I sighed, wondering what Luke would do if he actually caught up with Bobby. "I just hope they come back soon."

This detour was *not* in the green folder, and we now only had thirty minutes to get downtown and find parking before our *Spin* photo shoot.

"Dang!" Reggie brought his hand to his mouth as Luke grabbed Bobby by the scruff of his leather vest. He dragged him off the driveway, and they both fell into the nearby bushes.

Honestly, what was the point in lending him a clean shirt if he was just gonna roll around on the ground?

Reggie looked over his shoulder with a smirk. "Five bucks says Luke *clobbers* him."

"What? No way it's going to get to that point."

"I'm going to make sure neither of them does something they regret."

"Wait, Reggie!" I threw my arms up, then brought

them down. They hit the pleather seats with a loud slap. "Okay. Does anyone care if we're on time?"

I jogged across the street after my bandmates and found our guitarists wrestling across the lawn while Reggie half-heartedly tried to intervene.

"Dude, I'm trying to help!" Bobby yelped.

"Give it to me!" Luke said, pinning Bobby to the ground.

"Guys, I'm not loving this vibe." Reggie picked out some grass clippings from Luke's shaggy hair as he rolled by.

"You're gonna rip the shirt even more," I said, wincing as the frayed shoulder caught on a stray twig poking out from one of the bushes. We didn't have time to factor in a wardrobe change today. But Luke wasn't listening. "You *do* realize we have to be photo ready in less than a half hour?"

"Okay, fine! You can have the tickets." Bobby released the envelope from his grip. It fell to the grass, looking more tattered than ever. "Alex is right—it's *your* call. But just so we're clear, I was seriously only trying to help."

"Duh." Luke snatched the tickets off the lawn and crawled away from Bobby. He leaned back on his elbows, closing his eyes as he caught his breath in the afternoon sun. "Just give me time. I don't wanna mess this up, you know?"

The sound of the front door opening snapped our attention back to the house. I crouched to the ground so that *whoever* it was didn't see me. I gripped Reggie by the bottom of his leather jacket, bringing him down to hide with the rest of us.

But rather than hiding, Reggie crawled on all fours and sidled up to the bushes. He poked his head just above the leaves, then looked back at Luke and whispered, "Your mom's coming."

Prying the thick leaves apart with my fingers, I caught sight of Mrs. Patterson walking toward us. She looked exactly how I remembered her, with her brown hair falling just beneath her shoulders and her clunky garden clogs that she wore everywhere but the garden. Her gaze wandered over to the hedgerow, and I tugged on Reggie's jacket so that he would duck below the line of sight.

"She's coming this way. And she's gonna see me looking like *this*." Luke folded his arms around his knees, shaking his head. "This is *not* how I wanted this to go down."

"What are these flowers called?" Reggie stuck his face farther into the bushes, breathing in the scent of the white flowers. "They smell *wonderful*."

"Reggie, shush!" I whispered, though it came out

more like a hiss. I turned back to see Luke's mom taking a seat behind the station wagon's wheel. I gripped Luke's shoulder firmly, getting his attention. "She's leaving. It's now or never, man."

This was not the time to be paralyzed by pride and indecision. If Luke wanted to give her tickets to tonight's show, he'd have to do it fast. The rickety old Volvo roared to life and rocked forward, like Mrs. Patterson had shifted the gear into drive.

"I'm not just gonna jump out of the bushes and say, *'Surprise, Mom! Did ya miss me?'*"

"That wouldn't be the best look," Reggie agreed seriously, and Bobby hunched over, covering his mouth to muffle his laugh.

Luke's lips twitched as he fought a smile.

The station wagon lumbered down the driveway and slowed before turning onto the street, driving in the opposite direction of our parked van. Luke hopped up, pursing his lips as he looked down at Bobby. After a moment he held his hand out for him to take. He heaved Bobby into a standing position, his jaw tight, and then he clapped him on the shoulder.

"Tomorrow—after we've crushed our show at the Orpheum—I'll come see my mom. But this time, it'll be on *my* terms."

13

Julie

I left Flynn at her house, hoping that she could survive her mom's tofu onslaught for a couple more hours until dinnertime. When I got home, Carlos was in the front yard, dressed in his striped baseball pants and numbered jersey, which I recognized as his game day uniform. He swung his bat back and forth, practicing his form. He'd spent the entire week binge-watching baseball movies to work on his game. Now he was up to bat.

But first, it's time for a little payback.

I raised my white garment bag in front of me, wiggling it above the bushes so that it looked like a ghost.

"BOO!" I boomed from behind him in my best demon voice.

"AHHHHH!" he yelped, dropping the bat on the grass.

"Vengeance is mine!" I threw my head back in a cackle, quite pleased with myself. I grabbed his shoulders and rattled his stance. "Admit it. You thought I was a ghost, didn't you?"

"No, I didn't," he said, stamping his foot like a little kid. "I wasn't scared. I'm not scared of anything."

"Not *anything*?" I asked, folding my arms. When he shook his head, I asked, "What about homework?"

"Okay, maybe." He laughed, conceding. "By the way, Mom wanted to talk to you when you got back."

"Where is she?" I was eager to show her my new dress—*the* dress.

"She went upstairs to take a nap like an hour ago. She might be up now, though."

Taking the stairs two at a time, the dress bag bumped up and down in my arms as I rushed to show my mom. I made it to the second landing in less than a minute, then opened my parents' door slowly. If my mom was still sleeping, I didn't want to wake her.

Aunt Victoria had left, but the smell of nail polish and acetone still lingered in the air. And my mom's pedicure bucket was still set underneath her bedside chair. Thankfully she was awake, propped up by a pile of pillows while she sorted through a handful of mail. I knocked softly on the doorframe, and she looked up with a soft smile.

"Hey, chica." She waved me over.

I slid some of the discarded envelopes to the side and sat next to her, folding the garment bag into my lap. Her bed was a mess of papers—quinceañera catalogs, venue brochures, and unsorted mail. And her laptop was open and resting on her lap. It didn't look restful at all.

"I thought you were supposed to be taking a nap."

"I tried, but there's just so much to do!" She slapped the sea of catalogs around her, making them bounce. Then she gripped her temples with both of her hands. "Algun día voy aprender a tomar un día libre."

"I don't think you even know what a day off is, let alone how to take one." I laughed, but then I was distracted by something on the bed. "Oh, I like this one." I grabbed a sample invitation, feeling the filigree underneath my fingers.

"Isn't it pretty? It reminded me of you when I saw it," Mom said, sighing with satisfaction. She pointed to my dress bag. "What's that?"

I hopped up, eager to show my mom what Flynn and Misha had picked out. I laid the bag across my mom's legs and unzipped it, parting the two sides to reveal my dream dress. Mom's breath hitched as she caught sight of the beadwork, and her hand immediately shot out to trace the intricate stitching and pearls.

"Flynn's mom brought it home from her shop. She pulled it as soon as it arrived so that no one could buy it before I saw it."

"Jules." She looked up from the dress and into my eyes, her lip trembling. She put her hand on my arm. "Can I see it on?"

I nodded, and she sprang into action, ripping away her covers and jumping out of bed. She gathered the dress in her hands and ushered me into her bathroom. I closed the door and changed quickly—I was as excited as she was, and I couldn't wait to see what the dress looked like on *me*.

For months I'd been hoping to find my quinceañera dress—and hoping that Carrie would help me shop for one. I loved all the stuff at Misha's shop, but Carrie was able to get into the coolest boutiques in Beverly Hills and Malibu since her dad was a famous musician. And I guess I felt like I had to pick a dress from one of those fancy, exclusive shops to be noticed—particularly by Nick. Like, after seeing me in an expensive and over-the-top dress, he'd fall head over heels for me. And maybe a girls' day out with Carrie was all it would take to get our friendship back on track.

I should have known better.

But now that I had a dress that was so me—picked out by my ride-or-die best friend—my vision for my quinceañera had shifted. Those other people didn't matter, and I didn't have to be fancy to impress anyone. All that mattered now was how I felt in *this* dress.

I hope it fits!

I couldn't quite reach the back zipper, so I opened the bathroom door and asked for a little help. Mom was right on the other side of the door, waiting not-so-patiently to see the dress, and she pulled the zipper up, sniffling under her breath. Grabbing my shoulders, she guided me to the full-length mirror, which hung on the back of the door.

I inhaled sharply as I turned from side to side, listening to the layers of tulle swish against the carpet. The skirt looked so delicate compared to the bodice, which really upped the ante with its swirls of pearls and dark sequins. I looked like a glammed-up, rock-and-roll goddess.

This is my quinceañera dress.

"Di algo, mami. Don't you love it? Yes or yes?"

Mom wiped underneath both eyes with her fingers. "I can't wait to see you dance in it, to see you sing in it."

"We'll sing some of our songs."

"Promise?" Her nose twitched as she let out a little sob.

"Don't cry, because then I'll cry, too." My lip was already trembling, and I knew I couldn't take much more of Mom's tears before I burst into my own. We were two sides of the same coin.

Holding out her hand, she grabbed mine and twirled me around, and all of a sudden, I felt like I was six years old in my first poufy dress. I'd insisted on wearing it almost every day, and my mom would spin me in circles, over and over again until I got dizzy and collapsed on the ground in a pool of giggles.

This afternoon was no different.

After a few turns around the room, I dropped to the edge of my parents' bed, my vision slightly, delightfully blurred. When my eyes refocused, my mom's notebook caught my attention.

"What's this?" I peeked at the page. It was something I'd never seen before. "'Wake Up.' Are you working on a new song?"

"Honey, I'm *always* working on another song." She laughed. "This one is something special. I can just feel it. But it needs a lot of work—much more than *our* song."

"I think I have something for our untitled masterpiece, by the way." I tucked my hair behind my ear and knelt down for my backpack, digging for the scrap paper in the front pocket. "I thought of it when I was at Flynn's."

"Give it a go." Mom waved her hands excitedly as she sat on the edge of her bed.

"Without music?" I wasn't sure if my voice could fully carry the song a capella. Singing without my piano always made me feel too raw—bared for all to see.

"Don't be bashful. You sing from your soul, tu alma, from right here, mija." She patted her chest, right over her heart. "It's just you and me."

"Okay. Here it goes." I let out a heavy sigh and sank into the spot beside her, looking down at the page. The strength of the words hit me as I skimmed the lyrics again. I'd channeled my defiant spirit into these lines— all my frustration and sadness about Carrie, my stress from starting at a new school, and my dead-end crush on Nick. I channeled it into this song because I could always find comfort in my music. "This is what I was thinking we could do for the pre-chorus."

And it's one, two, three, four times
That I'll try for one more night
Light a fire in my eyes
I'm going out of my mind

"That's my girl!" Mom clapped her hands, her eyes brimming with pride. She bounced off the bed, even more energized than she had been moments ago. She yanked my dad's ukulele off the top of his dresser, and plucked the tiny strings, giving me backup music. "Let's start from the top."

Don't blink
No, I don't want to miss it
One thing
And it's back to the beginning
'Cause everything is rushing in fast
Keep going on, never look back

"And then the new pre-chorus!" I jumped off the bed and joined Mom on the other side of the room.

And it's one, two, three, four times
That I'll try for one more night
Light a fire in my eyes
I'm going out of my mind

"See? I told you—*anything* is possible if you put your mind to it. This song is going to be incredible once we finish it." Then my mom's eyes widened with mischief. "I have an idea. Come with me to the studio."

Reggie

By the time we arrived at *Spin* magazine, the air between Luke and Bobby remained a little tense. Luke was clearly still thinking about the close encounter at his parents' house, preferring to stay a few paces behind the rest of us as we walked through the sliding doors of the California Plaza tower in downtown Los Angeles—or DTLA as us *insiders* called it. The sound of our footsteps echoed off the walls of the huge lobby as we approached the receptionist's desk. A guy in a tailored black suit greeted us by holding up a finger.

"Please hold," he said into his headset. He typed something into his computer, then looked at me over the rim of his glasses. "Name?"

"Reggie Peters's the name, and playing bass is my

game," I said with a smirk. I looked around at my boys, who were varying degrees of *meh*. The receptionist blinked at me, expressionless.

Geez. Tough crowd, am I right?

"We're Sunset Curve," Alex said, stepping forward. He riffled through the pages of our worn band folder and pulled out a sheet of paper with our photo shoot information on it. "We're here to see Bernadette Read at *Spin*."

"Thank you." The receptionist plucked the sheet of paper out of Alex's hands and entered the data into his computer. Without looking at us, he said, "Okay, you're checked in. Take the elevator to the twelfth floor."

"So, what kind of vibe are we going for when we take this picture?" I hopped in front and turned to face the guys, walking backward on our way to the elevators. I smiled wider, trying to defuse the tension. "I, for one, am partial to the jumping-in-midair shot."

"That may be a little too cheesy." Alex pressed the button for the elevator. "I think we should go for the *brooding up-and-comer* look."

"That won't be hard," Bobby joked, looking at Luke out of the corner of his eye.

Luke's scowl deepened, and by the time we were zooming up to the twelfth floor, he looked downright miserable. I hoped he could turn that frown upside down—and *soon*. We were about to sit for our first official interview and professional photo shoot, and I wanted us to look good for our debut.

You know—for the ladies.

That's one of the perks of being in a rock band. You get to meet swarms of girls who are interested in your music—the most important part of you. I'd devoted countless days and weeks and hours to practicing my craft, developing my own sound so that I could raise my music to the next level. I did that because I *love* the bass. My instrument is a part of my body, and without it, I'd feel incomplete.

Again, I also did it for the ladies.

And there was a really cute one when we stepped off the elevator. I lunged in front of my bandmates—no sense in letting their sourpusses be the first of Sunset Curve she sees.

"It's so good to meet you." She held her hand out and shook vigorously, her short brown hair bobbing through the motion. "I'm Paige, Bernadette's assistant. I'll be stepping in for her today."

"Oh?" Luke piped up. It was the first thing he'd said in a while. "Is she not interviewing us?"

"She can't be here for an actual interview. That's

why she mailed you those questionnaires. Did you bring those with you?" Her eyebrows creased, as if it was self-evident that the interviewer would not be showing up to the interview. We obviously had a lot to learn about the music biz.

Alex handed her our worksheets, which we'd filled out beforehand. They were comprised of pretty basic questions like what our names were, where we were born, our favorite bands, and how long we'd been playing music. If I'd have known this was the entire basis of the interview, I would have spent more time on it instead of hastily jotting down my responses this morning. I was determined to make a deeper impression on Paige so that she could tell her boss we were something special.

And who knows? Maybe I'd get a date out of it.

She didn't look much older than us. And she was just so pretty and nice, and I bet she was smart, too—I could tell by the way she held her clipboard that she knew her way around a textbook. I mean, girls were all sorta amazing in their own way, and let's face it, I was kinda klutzy and slightly awkward, so I couldn't afford to be choosy. I was an equal opportunity lover—open to any takers.

"We're ready for you in the back. If you'll follow me." She extended an arm down the hallway, which was decorated in enlarged photos of the magazine's most iconic issues. Pearl Jam, Nirvana, Counting Crows, Radiohead, Alanis Morissette—they were all there, watching us as we walked to the back studio.

"So, what did you think about our music?" I asked.

"Honestly, I haven't quite gotten a chance to listen to it. But my boss, who sent me to fact-check this piece, she really liked your stuff. Said she couldn't get it out of her head." She stopped in front of the last door on the left and gestured for us to pile in.

It was a pretty large studio with a wall of windows on the other side of the room and a table of snacks behind the photographer, who had bright lighting equipment set up in front of a white screen. He looked up from adjusting his lens to give us a quick nod. I couldn't believe all this was for us.

Especially that table filled with snacks. I crossed the room in a few long strides. My mouth watered at the spread, and I found myself wondering if we could break from the shoot before it even started. But before I could lift a sandwich to my mouth, the rest of the group joined me, deep in discussion.

"Have you been at the magazine for long?" Luke raised his eyebrow skeptically, no doubt wondering if our article was being handled by a professional.

"Oh, no. I'm technically an intern. Working here for college credit." She gave an awkward grin but composed herself, straightening her posture and jutting her chin out. "I hope to work here once I graduate."

"Which will be in how many years?" I rubbed my chin, trying to look casual as I tried to calculate her *exact* age.

"Three?" She said it more like a question than with conviction.

If she was a freshman in college, that meant that she was basically our age, which meant I had a chance. And since she was seriously cute, I planned to make my move.

"Maybe you and I could grab some coffee and talk about journalism sometime." I leaned against the craft services table. It shifted underneath me and scooted closer to the window with a loud screech. I stumbled grabbing the table for support before finding my footing again. I donned my most winning smile to cover up my folly. "I've always been super interested in magazines. Why read anything else, right?"

"Right." She gave a strained laugh. I couldn't tell whether she thought my confession of not being a reader was cool. But I couldn't help but tell the truth—I was an open book who didn't like books. Her eyes gave me a once-over. "How old are you again?"

"Seventeen, but I've been told I'm an old soul." I tore off a sprig of grapes and popped one into my mouth.

"Call me when you're older." She threw her head back, laughing heartily. She snorted at the end of her laugh, so she covered her mouth. It was cute. She stepped away and then stopped, turning to look over her shoulder. "Oh, and the food actually isn't for you guys. It's for the next band coming in. They're going to be *huge*. But you can have a few grapes, since you already touched them."

And with a wink, she returned to the shoot.

"I think she likes me." I rubbed my hands together, feeling like a new man. I couldn't say the same for the rest of the bunch. Bobby looked deflated, Alex looked checked out, and Luke looked like a sick puppy.

Geez, guys.

I cleared my throat, grabbing their attention. "May I remind you that today is the day we reach legendary status?"

"With the intern?" Alex rolled his eyes.

"Nah, man. It's all on us." I ran my fingers through my hair, exhaling deeply. "Come on, guys. We can't keep clashing like this, or we'll literally end up like The Clash—broken up and not making music. Do you want that?"

"No." Alex shook his head quickly. "I *live* for this band."

"Me too," Bobby said, nodding slowly. "Luke, I really am sorry. I shouldn't have pushed you to talk to your mom."

"I'm not mad at you, Bobby." Luke sighed. "Guess I kinda needed a kick in the pants. I'm madder at myself for not actually talking to her."

"But you will tomorrow?" Bobby raised an eyebrow, looking skeptical and hopeful at the same time.

"I will, I promise. But right now we need to focus on us. Our band is *everything* to me. And I don't want anything to come between us and crushing it on that stage tonight." Luke uncrossed his arms and lifted his hands, his fingers twiddling in the air. "Can't you feel the energy in the air, boys? That's the universe telling us this is our time. I can feel it in my bones—can't you?"

I gulped. The hair on my arms started to rise. I *could* feel it in my bones—this urgency of living life to the fullest *right now.*

"Guys?" Paige raised her voice. Our heads snapped up to find her standing next to the photographer. "We're ready for you."

"So, does this mean the band's back?" I asked eagerly, drawing in the boys for a hug.

"Yes, okay! Yes." Alex's shoulders rumbled through a chuckle.

"Now that everyone's in a better mood, I'd like to revisit that jumping photo idea."

"Fine, but just *one*. We're trying to look like serious artists here." Luke grabbed my shoulders, his smile returning to his face. "And hey, thanks for bringing the bigger picture back into focus, Reg."

Once we were in front of the camera, the process didn't take long. Luke—thank *goodness*—didn't frown in every frame. Alex's typical charm was on full display, and Bobby's toothy grin was more grin, less teeth. As for me—I usually find it hard to hold a pose for a long time, but this was a different situation. Paige kept looking at me from the other side of the camera, and that made me smile.

After a few more shots, it was a wrap, and the photographer's team was already rearranging the set for a new band—probably the one who was important enough to have a snack table—before we even left the room. But that didn't change the importance of this moment for me. I was proud—no one in my family had ever been to a photo shoot before.

My brother, Steve, was possibly even more excited to see my face featured in a magazine than I was. Not to brag, but I was sorta his role model. The truth was, though, I usually spent more time with the band than I did with him, leaving my little brother to deal with our arguing parents by himself.

Yeah, I felt guilty about that sometimes.

But soon, all that time away from Steve will have been worth it. Now I had something to show for myself—professional band photos, a magazine article, *and* a showcase at one of LA's hottest venues. Finally, I felt like I was worthy of Steve's admiration. I couldn't wait to show him the proofs.

Get it? Show him *proof*?

Sometimes I crack myself up.

The rustling of papers nearby snapped my attention back to the present. I snapped my head to the edge of the craft services table, where Paige was trying to stuff more papers into her already-stuffed clipboard. Her cheeks reddened—just like mine do all the time—and I felt even more drawn to her.

I wanted to leave Paige with a parting gift, something to remember the brief but memorable time we'd spent together. I'd give her one of our band T-shirts, like I did to all of my potential love interests. So far, I'd given out *a lot* of shirts and—can you believe it?— received no calls back.

But when did that ever stop me?

"Guys, who brought the T-shirts?" I asked over my shoulder as I wrote my phone number on a paper napkin. The only response I got was empty stares.

I had a sinking feeling in my gut. This time, I knew it wasn't hunger pangs.

"I think Luke was right earlier. We *did* forget something." I felt a scarlet blush creep across my face. "We forgot to pick up the T-shirts to sell at the show!"

Julie

My mom gripped the railings of the steep steps up to the loft above the garage studio. When she got to the top, she heaved herself onto the landing and sat on the edge of it. Her legs dangled over the ladder.

"I haven't been up here in ages," she said, a little out of breath. She smiled down at me, her black curls falling around her face. She folded her legs underneath her, then heaved herself up into a standing position. "Come on up."

I hopped up the stairs and was at the top within moments. My mom had made it look hard, but it was a piece of cake. She looked at me, her face flushed.

"Oh, to be young again," she said wistfully.

"Mom, you *are* still young. Aren't you only like

fifty?" I covered my mouth, stifling a laugh. I knew my mom was younger than that, but I couldn't help but tease her a little.

"Ouch. I'm not *that* old." She gripped her chest as if she was offended, but then a smile crept across her face. She opened her arms wide, looking over her shoulder. "This is the rock-and-roll graveyard your aunt was talking about."

"She wasn't lying," I mumbled as I strolled through the cluttered space. Stacks of CDs towered in a corner, toppling into a mound of folders and papers. It was hard to see where one mess ended and another began. In another corner lay an old fender and a dusty electric keyboard. It looked *ancient*, like it hadn't been played in decades. "Is all this yours?"

"Goodness no." She shook her head and knelt down to a cardboard box at her feet. "Most of this stuff was here when we bought the house. That sometimes happens when you buy a property as is. You inherit another person's hoard."

"Whoever lived here before really knew their music." I riffled through handwritten sheet music strewn over a plastic card table. Most of it was finished, and from what I could read, the music was interesting. A large covered heap behind the table caught my attention. I slid the sheet covering off it, revealing a round drumhead. "Is this a complete drum set?"

Mom was a talented musician—a phenom on the piano and decent on any other instrument she picked up. But I'd never heard of her playing the drums. They looked so out of place in our studio.

"I think so." Mom stopped rummaging and looked up. "More of the musician's hoard."

"Don't tell Carlos." I laughed. If he saw these vintage drums, he'd surely want to start taking lessons. My ears throbbed just *thinking* about the racket.

"It'll be our little secret." She stood up, holding an armful of rope and bungee cords in her hands.

"What is that for?"

"Es para nuestro proyecto. Our secret project," she said, her mischievous smile growing.

I didn't know what she was up to, but whatever it was, it was making her tired eyes glow with brightness. She tiptoed onto a faded rug, weaving around another pile of junk until she came to a stack of wooden chairs.

"This'll work." She patted the stack, sending a whirlwind of dust billowing into the air. She waved her hand in front of her face, coughing. "One of these days we gotta clean this place out."

Oh no. I hope that's not our fun project.

"How about never?" I smiled nervously, backing away from the clutter. I didn't want to be stuck up here, organizing someone else's mess. I'd lived here my whole life without ever feeling the need to come up here. We could leave this mess for another lifetime, as far as I was concerned.

Whoever had to clean out this studio would have a *lot* of work cut out for them.

"Let's get these downstairs." My mom shimmied the top chair loose from the stack, holding her head to the side to avoid the ensuing dust storm.

"Seriously, Mom." I placed my hands on my hips and cocked my head to the side. "What are you planning on doing with ropes and old wooden chairs?"

"Do you trust me?"

"Not sure right now." I pursed my lips, trying to look serious, but a laugh escaped my mouth. "Okay, fine. I trust you."

"I'll lower this first one to you. When it gets to the ground, untie the rope, and I'll bring it back up." She clapped her hands, rubbing them together. "Wash, then repeat."

I lowered myself onto the ladder and hopped down the steps two at a time, using gravity to assist me. From the lower level I yelled up. "Ready!"

"Anchors away!" my mom said, holding the chair over the railing. Slowly, she lowered it down, lengthening the rope with a measured pace. "Stand back, mija. I don't want you to get hurt."

The chair landed with a *clank* on the floorboards. I did as instructed and untied the rope from it. When I gave the tether a little tug, my mom pulled the rope back up. We did five or six rounds of this—her lowering, me untying and tugging, her pulling the rope back up. When I untied the last one, my mom joined me on the ground floor, and we were surrounded by a sea of wooden chairs.

"Soooo we're making an army of mismatched seats?" I frowned, more confused than ever. My mom had been *so* excited to come show me something out here. I thought the surprise was something better than throwaway furniture.

"We're going to put these"— she said, gripping the back of one of the chairs and then tilting her head up—"up there."

I followed her gaze to the top of the ceiling's tall rafters. I sputtered out a laugh. *"What?"*

"Get it? *Floating in the air, just like a chair.*" She opened her mouth wide, nodding slowly as if she'd just said the punch line of a joke. When I didn't respond, she said,

"It's from your lyrics this morning. It's a tribute to conquering our challenges, because *anything* is possible."

"That's a stretch. Are you sure you just didn't get the urge to do a little spring cleaning?"

"Maybe a little," she said, wiggling her nose. She tied the rope around the first chair and held out the coiled loops. "Come on. Humor me."

"You want me to throw it up there?" I looked at the ceiling again, which must have been twenty feet above our heads.

It took me several tries—hey, I never claimed to have a good throwing arm. But finally, we threaded the needle, tossing the rope over a wooden beam and watching it fall to the other side. Together we hoisted the chair above our heads until the chair hung flush with the ceiling.

Mom held the rope tight as she climbed the ladder again and secured it onto another rafter. Then she lumbered down and crossed the room to the couch. Grabbing a handful of pillows, she dropped them on the floor, scattering them at her feet.

"Time to gaze at our handiwork." She lowered to the ground. Resting her head on a pillow, she gazed at the oddity. I followed her lead, claiming the pillow next to her.

"It's kinda surreal," I whispered, feeling like I was in *Alice in Wonderland*, where up was down and down was up.

"Hey, it was sort of your idea." She turned her head, a soft smile on her lips.

"That was a line from a song. I didn't mean it literally."

"Well, I meant what I said." She grabbed my arm and squeezed it gently. "You can *literally* make your wildest dreams come true if you try really, really hard. With a little effort, we can breathe life into the impossible."

"I love that." I turned onto my back and looked at our masterpiece. Remembering the rest of the chairs, I gave her a sidelong glance. "We don't have to hang the rest today, do we?"

"We can conquer those another day," she said, her voice faint and sleepy.

I lay there for a while, thinking about our unfinished song and all the songs I'd yet to write. They formed in the shadows of my mind, waiting to be brought to light. And my mom made me think that was possible. The sky was the limit.

When I checked on her again, she was fast asleep, breathing slowly and softly. I was glad she was finally able to get the rest she'd been searching for all day. I grabbed the throw blanket off the couch, moving carefully so that I wouldn't make any noise. I draped it over her body, and she pulled it close before falling deeper into her long-awaited nap.

16

Luke

The van careened around the corner and sped down Hollywood Boulevard. It was crowded with tourists, as usual, but Bobby expertly wove through the traffic, past the weird street performers in front of the Hollywood Theater. This part of town was famous for its street buskers—out of work actors and musicians trying to make a buck by entertaining sidewalk spectators. Bobby pressed on the gas pedal, speeding past blocks of souvenir shops, street vendors, and even blowing through a yellow light to get us to the shop on time.

He pulled the minivan so close to the curb, the cement scratched the wheels. He winced at the sound as the van jolted to a stop. Alex quickly unbuckled his seat belt and knelt over the back seat to check to see if his drums were okay.

"My poor baby," he whimpered as he assessed the damage. He let out a sigh of relief, then slapped the back of the driver's seat. "You could have killed us, or *worse*— smashed our instruments."

"Come on, guys!" I jumped out of the car, waving for them to follow me, then sprinted down the block to find our shirt shop, Status Tees—the cheapest T-shirts around. It wasn't exactly convenient to drive to the most congested part of town to pick up our merchandise, but we had no choice. We couldn't afford anything else.

A wall of air-conditioning hit me when I opened the door. The store was crammed with racks of shirts and rows of fitted baseball caps—basically anything you wanted to print something on, this was the place to be.

Reggie and Alex rushed in shortly after, their hungry eyes scanning all the possibilities in the shop. But I was not as easily distracted. I looked at the clock above the shopping clerk's head. It was already half past four, and we needed to be at the Orpheum Theater, set up for sound check, at six. We'd be cutting it close.

Too close.

"Hi, my name is Luke Patterson," I said to the sales associate, wiping my sweaty forehead with the back of my arm. "I'm here to pick up a box of shirts for Sunset Curve."

"You guys got here *just* in time. We close at five today." He pushed his tinted glasses up the bridge of his nose, then gathered his long blond hair into a ponytail. "Lemme go grab that from the back," he said before disappearing into the storeroom behind the counter.

I slumped against the glass display case, catching my breath as relief washed over me. I watched Reggie peruse a rack of fitted caps. He plucked a yellow Lakers hat from the top shelf and put it on, checking himself out in the mirror.

"What do you think? Can I pull it off?" He turned his head from side to side, modeling it for me.

"No, but I think I might be a fedora guy." Alex popped out of one of the aisles in a tan straw hat. He framed his face with his hands. "Pretty great, huh?"

"We'll have to have a band meeting about hats." I chuckled against the counter.

When I heard footsteps from the storeroom, I heaved myself into a standing position. Toting a large cardboard box in his arms, the salesman emerged behind the counter and placed it on the glass top.

"All right, that'll be a hundred bucks," he said, checking the invoice taped to the top of the box.

"A *hundred dollars*?" I felt my face flush as I spun around to face Alex. "I thought you said these were cheap."

"They *are* cheap—like forty percent less than all the other places I checked." Alex jutted his chin out, defending his calculations. "We talked about this."

I racked my brain for the conversation and vaguely remembered discussing the pros and cons of buying merch. We'd all agreed to chip in, but that was before we blew most of our money on Foo Fighters tickets and gas for Bobby's van. A knot of fear twisted in my chest as I slowly realized we might not have enough to cover the shirts.

"Can I borrow that pen?" I asked. The surly dude nodded in permission. I tore off a sticky note and hovered the pen over the page. I looked to Reggie first. "How much do you have?"

"I've got fifteen dollars and . . ." He paused as he fished for change in his back pocket. He set a fistful of coins on the counter and sifted through, counting under his breath. "And twenty-eight cents."

I grumbled.

"What? I bought a *lot* of pens. And those aren't cheap, you know." Reggie popped a grape into his mouth.

Wait. Where did he get more food?

I sighed. We were totally screwed if we kept producing such low numbers.

"Here's forty dollars and nineteen cents from me." Alex piled his money on top of Reggie's crumpled bills. He dug into another pocket and produced another wad of cash. "And here's thirty-two bucks from Bobby. He's waiting by the car."

"And I've got eight dollars." I scribbled down my contribution, a tad embarrassed by how small it was, then added up the amounts.

Geez, I wish I paid more attention in math class instead of writing songs during it.

"Oh, wow. We're close. We're at ninety-five dollars and forty-seven cents." I double-checked my math, just to make sure we were within striking distance of the price tag. Sure enough, it added up. I bobbed my head, seriously proud of us. "That's basically the full cost."

"Basically?" The salesclerk raised his eyebrows.

"Is there any way you could take out a couple shirts and only charge us for the ones left in the box?" I asked, clasping my hands together.

"That's a no-go, bro." He waved his arms and scoffed. "What am I gonna do with a bunch of Sunset Swerve shirts?"

"Sunset *Curve*," I said, unsurprised to hear Reggie and Alex correct the clerk at the same time. We'd worked hard to find the perfect band name, and we wanted everyone to know who we were.

The sales guy pursed his lips, looking completely uninterested in the name of our band. Alex held his hands up, a deep red blush creeping across his face. "Okay, sorry. I get it. No discount on the shirts."

"No can do." He shook his head slowly. "No money, no shirts."

"Wait." I looked at the clock and then back at the street where Bobby was waiting. We couldn't go to the theater empty-handed, especially since we were *so* close to getting everything we wanted. "We'll figure something out. I just need time to think."

"Whatever, man." The sales associate sat on a stool and pulled out a comic book from underneath the counter. He held a fist up in solidarity. "Power to you. Just know, we close in twenty minutes."

Adrenaline spiked my veins as I digested that information. How were we going to get five dollars before the store closed? We couldn't ask our families for help. They lived on the other side of town and we were short on time. And there was no way the diner would give me another advance on my paycheck.

This can't be happening.

Shoving off the counter, I joined Alex and Reggie near the front display window to regroup. I paced the small space, hoping an angel would drop the money right in my lap. In the anxious quiet, the bustle of the street filled the void while we searched for a way to come up with the deficit.

"I'm not above begging for it." Reggie gripped the lapels of his leather jacket and took a deep breath, eyeing each passerby—probably trying to muster the courage to ask them for money.

The music from one of the street performers caught my ear—a man playing his guitar on the sidewalk, his gravelly voice traveling down Hollywood Boulevard. A woman threw a few coins in his upturned hat as she passed by.

An idea slowly started to form.

"That's it." I grabbed Reggie by the collar as adrenaline surged through my veins. "We're going to work for that money. Doing what we do best—*singing. For tips.* Just like we've done at the pier a million times."

"But we've already practiced." Alex looked worried as he brought his hand up to his neck. He rubbed his throat, right where his vocal cords were. "Don't you want to keep your voice fresh for tonight?"

"Does anyone have a better idea?" I raised my eyebrows, searching both of their faces. "Look, all we need is four bucks and some change."

"In less than twenty minutes." Alex sighed.

"So, let's put on a show these people won't soon forget." I clapped my hands, feeling pumped. We could make that money in no time. Today was our day, and I believed in my boys.

Alex gulped, looking wary, but Reggie wrapped his arm around Alex's shoulders.

"Come on, live a little." He shook him, rattling his rigid stance. "Let's live like there's no tomorrow."

Bobby

I waited in the car to make sure it didn't get towed while the guys were in the store. Technically, I was in a no-parking zone, so a cop *could* give me a ticket at any moment. But that had never stopped me before. When you drove around LA in a bulky minivan, sometimes you had to get creative with where you parked.

Leaning against the steering wheel, I watched a musician perform on the sidewalk. He played his guitar with masterful ease, changing chords at the drop of a dime. His scratchy voice reminded me of Tom Waits, and it mixed well with his staticky amp. He was pretty good, and that fact was evident in the decent-size crowd that grew by the minute. I almost lost myself in the show, but then I remembered we had our own to do.

What's taking the guys so long?

They'd been in the shop for a while, so I knew something was up. It shouldn't have taken longer than a few minutes to pick up a box of shirts, right? I was on borrowed time in this parking spot. My hands started to sweat as I gripped the steering wheel tighter.

Luke burst through the shop doors with Alex and Reggie at his heels. Their eyes were bright, and they all had this determined look on their faces like they were ready for something *big*. The only thing they didn't have was that box of shirts.

What are they up to now?

I wish I knew what it was. Sometimes I felt like I was on the edge of the group, kept at arm's length. I was part of the group but still *apart*.

"Small snag in our plans. We're a little short on cash, so we couldn't buy the shirts—*yet*." Luke threw open the side door and grabbed his guitar out of the back seat. "We have twenty minutes to make five bucks."

"We're taking our beats to the streets," Reggie beamed, holding his hand out for a high five. I leaned over the van's center console and tapped his hand. "That's the spirit."

"Alex, you *cannot* take your drums out of the car," I

said out of the driver's side window, tapping the clock on the dashboard to remind him of the time. It had taken us forever to squeeze them into the back. "We're already cutting it close as it is."

"He's got a point." Alex looked at Luke, his eyebrows upturned.

"Don't stress. I got it covered. Grab your sticks." Luke smirked, waving away Alex's worries with a stroke of his hand. He poked his head back in the van, grabbing the handle of my guitar case. "You can leave the car to play one song."

I turned the car off and joined them on the sidewalk. Luke handed me my guitar.

"All right, guys, we got this." Luke put his hand on my and Reggie's shoulders, drawing the group into a huddle for one of his pep talks—like a coach might have with his team before a big game. "Just think of this as another practice. It can only make us stronger."

Ah, Luke. The eternal optimist when it came to Sunset Curve.

Reggie bobbed up and down on his heels, ready to get started. If Luke was our coach, then Reggie was our mascot, and Alex—the ever-reasonable planner—was the team manager.

Sorry to bring up another sports analogy, but I can't help it.

Outside of band stuff, I was surrounded on all sides by sports. My older brothers hit the trifecta of school sports, covering all the bases—basketball, football, and baseball. And who was I on Sunset Curve's all-star team?

I was second-string.

Sure, I added dimension to our sound by playing the harmony to Luke's melody, but technically they didn't need another guitarist. Reggie had the bass covered, and Alex was masterful behind his drum set. I wasn't even great with lyrics—that was Luke all the way. But I had a van that could take us places, and hey—my harmony and transportation capabilities (plus years of friendship) were enough to keep me around.

We broke from our huddle, and Luke headed straight for the trash bin next to the bus stop. He knotted the top of the bag, then lifted it out of the container. Turning it upside down, he slapped the top.

"Drums!" He smiled at Alex. "Okay, boys. 'Now or Never.'"

We hadn't played a single note before the other street performer interrupted us. He rushed into the middle of our circle, his eyebrows furrowed. "Hey, what do you think you're doing? This is my corner!"

"We only need five bucks in the next fifteen minutes." I stepped forward. I felt like I knew the guy better than the others, since I'd been watching him play while the guys were in the T-shirt shop. He was a masterful performer. "I have a proposition for you. Can we share your corner?"

"What's the split?" he asked, followed by a raspy sigh. "How much do I get out of it, kid?"

"Anything beyond what we need," Luke said.

"And I'll throw in a T-shirt." Reggie smiled, pointing to the shop behind us. "Fresh off the presses."

"It's a deal." The older musician stepped to the side, ceding the sidewalk to us.

"Here we go." Luke kicked open his guitar case and positioned it in the middle of the sidewalk so that people could give us tips.

"One, two, three!" Alex counted off, spurring us into action.

Luke raised his voice to sing. Without the help of a microphone to boom his voice over the street noise, he belted louder than I'd ever heard him.

Take off
Last stop
Countdown 'til we blast open the top

143

Face-first
Full charge
Electric hammer to the heart

Clocks move forward
But we don't get older, no
Kept on climbing
'Til our stars collided

And all the times we fell behind
Were just the keys to paradise

Don't look down
'Cause we're still rising
Up right now
And even if we
Hit the ground
We'll still fly
Keep dreaming like we'll live forever
But live it like it's now or never

He swung his head back, flicking his hair—and the sweat along with it! That earned a gasp from the crowd. A few coins fell into the hat on the sidewalk.

I jumped into the middle of the sidewalk, right in front of a passing gaggle of girls—seriously *cute* girls with butterfly clips in their hair. I winked, trying to keep them interested in our public display of rock and roll.

Hear the noise
In my head
It's calling out like a voice I can't forget

One life
No regrets
Catch up, got no time to catch my breath

Clocks move faster
'Cause it's all we're after now

Won't stop climbing
'Cause this is our time, yeah
When all the days felt black and white
Those were the best shades of my life

Don't look down
'Cause we're still rising
Up right now
And even if we
Hit the ground
We'll still fly
Keep dreaming like we'll live forever
But live it like it's now or never

Luke hopped onto the bus stop bench, teetering on the tips of his toes as he commanded the crowd's attention. He played with gusto on a good day because he believed that every show had the ability to propel our band into the stratosphere. Whether we were playing in a small venue or in our garage studio, he belted out our beats with fierce conviction—even if it meant that the owners of the studio had to ask us to lower the volume—and our sidewalk concert was no different.

This was why I'd wanted to join the band. The way he looked up to Dave Grohl was the way I looked up to Luke. I always had—even when we were kids. He just seemed to operate on a higher frequency, and I wanted to be on that level, too.

I'd be lying if I said I was anywhere near as good as he was, and that sorta bugged me, because we'd picked up the guitar around the same time. But it was just a fact, and everyone knew it. Anyone who saw Luke perform knew he was *going places*.

Sunset Curve was going places.

And as long as they let me be in the band, I'd ride their coattails to the top.

My hand plunged into the guitar case and scooped up the wrinkled wad of cash. I sorted through it quickly, making stacks of coins on the concrete as I tallied the dollars.

"We made almost twice as much as we need." I folded the five dollars we needed and handed it to Luke, who threw his head back with a howl.

"What did I tell you, boys? This is *our day*." He cackled, his eyes lit up with excitement. "The universe is clearly on our side. We're unstoppable."

He bolted toward the T-shirt shop door. I checked my Casio watch, breathing a sigh of relief. We'd made all the money we needed with one minute to spare.

"I'll get this stuff back in the car." Alex placed Luke's guitar back in its case and snapped it shut. He held his hand out to take mine, too.

"Thanks, man." I pulled the strap over my head, and he zipped it up in the cloth case. He and Reggie headed to the van, and I stayed behind to settle up with the street performer.

"A deal's a deal," I said, placing the rest of the money in his outstretched hat. He nodded in thanks and turned to leave, but I stopped him. "I was listening to you play earlier. You're amazing on the strings."

"Been playing most of my life. I was like you kids

once—doing whatever I could to play a show." He shook his head as if that time was long gone. "Where was it you said you were playing tonight?"

"The Orpheum."

"*Ahh,* named after Orpheus, the guy who went to Hades to save his girl." He chuckled when I scrunched up my face. "It's from Greek mythology."

"Never heard of him." I shrugged.

"One of the great tragedies. Orpheus never returned, got stuck in the underworld." He patted me on the shoulder. "Stay in school, kid. Learn something."

"Hey," I yelled after him. "What's your name?"

I figured it was about time I asked. It was the least I could do after he'd done us a solid and let us play on his corner.

"My name's Trevor," he said with a gruff, then shuffled down the street.

I turned the name around in my head, loving the edge it had to it. Maybe one day, when I made it big, I'd change my name to something like that—something better than Bobby Shaw.

18

Julie

While mom slept on the palette of pillows in the studio, I committed our new lyrics to the sheet music from this morning. Placing the notes in their rightful places was so satisfying. When I finished it, I held the pages and smiled at the *rightness* of the arrangement. A song was born!

Well . . . *almost*. We still needed a chorus to bring it all together. I was tempted to spit something out on the page, right then and there—maybe I could fit in something about *floating chairs* and *anything is possible*. But after messing around with several different options, I put my pen down. This song would not be finished today. Mom and I had loads of time to work on it. For now, I'd have to be content with what we had on the page.

And what we had on the page was *ahh*-mazing—to use one of Flynn's favorite terms.

I looked up to see Carlos, still dressed in his baseball uniform, sitting on the floor in front of the large flat screen watching another baseball movie. This time, it was *The Sandlot*—one of his new favorites. It made me briefly think of Flynn—the nineties seriously *were* making a comeback in my life. I wondered what other gifts from that time period would land on my doorstep.

The smell of pasta sauce wafted into the living room from the kitchen, where Dad was attempting to start dinner without Mom. His cooking skills weren't as good as my mom's, but he *was* learning under her tutelage. Ever the teacher, she guided him as she did all her students—with patience and perseverance.

"Ouch," my dad hissed from the stove, licking his finger like he'd just burned himself. "Don't worry. I'm okay."

I unfurled myself from my perch on the couch, prepared to lend him a hand, but my mom slid open the back door, her hair in a flurry from sleeping on the pillows in the studio. She rubbed her neck like she'd slept on it the wrong way.

"That might hurt in the morning," she said, coming over to give me a kiss on my forehead. "But I needed that. Thanks for letting me sleep."

Leaning against the kitchen island, she checked in on my dad to see if he needed help. But he gave her a thumbs-up. "This is going to be a five-star dinner. I just know it! A *delizioso* date night meal, right under our roof."

"I'll go change." She looked at her watch and tucked her curls behind her ear. "We'll leave here right after the kids finish dinner, okay? And, Carlos?"

"Huh?" he answered without turning away from the TV.

"Don't sit so close to the TV." She wagged her finger. "It's not good for your eyes."

The stairs creaked as she scampered up to her room to get ready for her night out with Dad. I settled back into the couch, watching the movie along with Carlos, who occasionally mumbled under his breath that he was going to be the next Great Bambino. The movie was halfway over when my mom reappeared in black jeans and a maroon blouse under her black leather jacket. She looked stunning.

"Wow, Mom." I sat up from the couch. "I thought you were lending that jacket to Tía."

"I wanted to wear it one last night before I parted with it. It's fun, right?" She gave a turn from side to side, modeling all angles for me. Then her nose perked up. Something was burning in the kitchen. She dashed over to my dad's side. "Did you stir it? You don't want to let the bottom burn."

I set the place mats around the table, one for each of us—Mom, Dad, me, and Carlos. Then I remembered my impromptu invite for Flynn. My head snapped in the direction of the kitchen, where my parents stood shoulder to shoulder over the stove.

"Can Flynn come over for dinner tonight?"

"Sure," Dad said absentmindedly as he shook a bottle of spices over the pot.

"If her mom says it's okay," Mom said as her hand shot out and stopped my dad's arm from shaking more of the spices in. He had a habit of being heavy-handed with ingredients. Mom brought out the finesse in his inner chef.

She brought the finesse out in us all.

I snagged another place mat from the cabinet in the kitchen island and scooted an extra chair over to the table.

"Carlos, come help me set the table," I yelled into the living room, where he'd inched closer to the TV when he thought no one was watching.

"Five more minutes," he mumbled over his shoulder, transfixed by the images on the screen.

"Mami," I turned to her for help, but her attention was pointed elsewhere. Her eyes were on my dad, who was wafting the fumes of pasta sauce toward his nostrils.

"¿Y ahora?" He dipped a wooden spoon into the saucepan and scooped up a mound of steaming red sauce.

Mom gave an indulgent smile and rested her hand gently over his. She poured some of the sauce out, leaving only a mouthful, over which she gently blew. After a few seconds, she took a tentative taste.

"I could watch you do that all day." My dad's eyes were wide—full of wonder at my mom.

Ugh, gross, they're so embarrassing.

"There are children present!" I rolled my eyes from the table. I was *so* not in the mood to watch my parents' PDA.

"Yeah, get a room!" Carlos squealed from across the room.

"Hey, don't you see how much I love your mother. Come here, mi amor." He snaked his arm around her waist and pulled her in for a featherlight peck on the lips.

I wanted to roll my eyes, but I couldn't. They were *super* cute. I could only hope to have the same thing with someone when I grew up. I thought briefly about

Nick. I had a serious crush on him, but my fantasies never reached further than holding hands and walking to class together. Was he really a dream come true?

I don't know. Maybe *that guy* was still out there for me.

Besides, Nick seemed more interested in Carrie than anyone else. And Carrie . . . well, she didn't seem to want anything to do with me anymore. I needed to stop checking my phone for a response from her because clearly she wasn't going to text or call me back. And as much as that fact pained me—and believe me, it *did*—I couldn't *make* anyone like me. I couldn't make her be my friend.

Maybe it was time to let both Carrie and Nick go. I'd leave the door open, but they couldn't steal my smile anymore. Not on a day like this—a day that was quickly becoming the *best day ever.*

My best friend had found me the perfect quinceañera dress, I wrote new lyrics with my mom, and I even hung a chair from the ceiling of the studio.

Honestly, I couldn't see how it could get any better than this.

"A good sauce takes patience, my love. But yes, this is ready to go." Mom rubbed her hands together. "Now, time for the pasta. Julie, would you—"

The front door flung open, and Flynn panted on the threshold like she'd run all the way from her house. I'd left the door unlocked, figuring she would do the same thing I always did when I went to her house—just let herself in. But I didn't expect her to make such a dramatic entrance.

But I should have known. There was never a dull moment with Flynn.

2019

19

Flynn

I stumbled into the Molinas' foyer and shut the door with a bang, a bit harder than I'd meant to. With my back flush against the door, my chest rising and falling in quick pants, I gripped my chest to slow my heart rate.

"Um . . . hey?" Julie tilted her head to the side, an invitation for me to tell her why I was out of breath.

"Oh, thank goodness." I looked over to the table, freshly set without the food on it. They hadn't started dinner without me. Julie raised an eyebrow.

I raised one back. *Can't a girl wanna eat?*

"Okay, fine. I narrowly escaped one of my mom's homemade mayo facials. I didn't want a redo of last time. You know, when it got stuck in my hair *and* caused me to break out into a million zits?" I shivered as I remembered the sound of cracked eggs and the emulsion blender. "My mom's theory: It was just the facial doing its job, lifting the *toxins* out of my skin. But my theory is: I don't wanna go down that road again. So, I ran, okay?"

Sometimes, you just gotta nope out.

Again, I had nothing but love for my parents, but when they missed the mark, they *really* missed the mark. Of course, Julie found it amusing. She was doubled over laughing, no doubt imagining my face coated in my mother's gooey concoction. I'd *love* to see her dodging poultices and meatless meat loaves on a regular basis.

She wouldn't last a day.

I shoved off the Molinas' door and bumped Julie out of the way with my hip as I made my way to the kitchen. Mr. Molina was literally watching the pot of hot water boil. He still had a lot to learn about cooking—least of which the first rule of *not watching a pot boil.* Julie's mom still had a lot of work cut out for her.

Poking my head between Julie's parents, I breathed in the scent of the simmering meat sauce. It smelled divine. This—*this* was what I'd been waiting for all afternoon while I'd been lumbering through my world history homework *on a Saturday.*

That's what I get for writing Double Trouble songs during the week, I guess.

Julie's dad cleared his throat, and I looked up at him.

"Don't mind me," I said breathlessly, pushing my musings aside. I sidestepped out of the way. "Smells delicious, though."

"You'll love my boiled salt water." Mr. Molina brought his fingers to his lips and gave them a dramatic chef's kiss. *"Magnifico."*

"I see I'm not the only one with weird parents," I said under my breath once I was by my best friend's side on the other side of the kitchen island. Mrs. Molina heard it and ruffled Julie's hair on her way to the kitchen counter.

"You gotta love them, though." Julie smiled as she watched her parents interact over the stove. They were still playful, sneaking kisses and swatting away silly jokes like they'd never grown out of their honeymoon phase. I loved seeing them together. Carlos made fake gagging noises, but I could tell he loved watching his parents in love, too.

"Yeah, they're pretty great," I said under my breath as I watched them.

"Here is the main event." Mrs. Molina carried a large bowl of pasta to the kitchen table, then doubled back to the stove for the sauce. Carefully, she poured the sauce over the noodles, then mixed it together with a pronged spaghetti spoon. Steam escaped the bowl, and I shamelessly leaned into the fumes.

"It's so beautiful, I could cry." My stomach grumbled in agreement.

"Dinner is served," Mr. Molina said, slinging his dishcloth over his shoulder.

After we said grace, everyone plunged their forks into the large bowl, instead of waiting for it to be passed around the table. This was being served family style, in every sense of the word. When I'd piled enough on my plate, I shoveled a couple bites into my mouth, feeling warmth wash over me. I was nearly finished with my serving when I noticed Julie's mom looked kinda dressed up.

"You look *very* fancy, Mrs. Molina," I said before shoving a heaping forkful in my mouth.

"That's because they have date night tonight." Julie rolled her eyes and shook her head.

"My parents do that, too! Are you guys going to an astrology seminar or a mixer at the science museum?" Carlos arched his eyebrow, gawking at me like I'd suggested something outlandish. I laughed into my cup of water. "What? That's what my parents consider romance."

"Everyone has their song to sing," Mrs. Molina said, putting her napkin up to hide her giggle. She and my mom had been friends as long as Julie and I had—since we were six. But they still had their differences, and my mom's love of the astral plane was one of them.

"We're going to the Dog Gone Lounge." Mr. Molina grinned at his wife from across the table.

"You're going to a concert?" I asked, remembering that my parents had gone to a show at that venue before. Well, it wasn't really a show—more like a slam poetry night with a lot of spoken word performances.

"Not exactly." Mrs. Molina bobbed her head from side to side, looking down at her plate. She took another bite of her food.

"Well, that's what you're going to get at the Dog Gone, *unless* . . ." My head snapped up. "Unless *you're* going to sing."

"Don't be ridiculous. My mom doesn't sing onstage anymore." Julie threw a piece of bread across the table at me, which earned a stern look from her dad and an *awesome* from Carlos. Her mom remained silent, biting her lips between her teeth. She had not contradicted me, and Julie had noticed. Her jawed dropped. "Wait. *What?*"

"It's nothing really." Mrs. Molina looked up from her plate, her eyebrows upturned. "It's just an open mic night."

"How often do you do stuff like this?" Julie asked, leaning forward.

"Sometimes I try out new material there." Mrs. Molina shrugged like this wasn't a big deal. But it totally was—she was getting back onstage again.

I didn't know what happened in the past and neither did Julie, but Mrs. Molina gave up on trying to be a performing musician. She became a music theory teacher and a piano tutor instead, but it was nice to see she'd never really given up on her dream.

We've all got a second act inside of us, right?

"You two should debut your new song there!" I swished my finger between Julie and her mom.

"Um, that's impossible, because it's not finished." Julie pursed her lips. "Remember, I told you it still needs a chorus."

"Okay, then what about 'Fueling the Fires'?" I suggested, throwing out another possibility. "That one's finished, and you *know* it's fire."

Mrs. Molina tilted her head and looked out the window, considering it. She squinted her eyes at Julie, a small smile creeping across her lips. "¿Sabes qué? That's actually not a bad idea. I thought we might perform it at your quinceañera, but it's begging to be sung sooner. And like I told you earlier—it's Hollywood club ready." She raised her eyebrows expectantly. "What do you say?"

"I, uh . . ." Julie huffed as she tried to find the words. She loved singing with her mom, but she found it harder to sing in front of a bunch of people—especially if she was singing her own lyrics. She was a perfectionist and was never *quite* ready to let go of her songs by making them public. Julie scrunched up her face. "Won't we be crashing your date night?"

"Not at all." Julie's dad shook his head, winking at his wife across the table. "Think of it as a special guest appearance."

"What do you think, Angel Face?" Mrs. Molina asked.

Julie looked around the table, then at me as I bounced in my seat. *Say yes*, I wanted to say. But Julie had to make this decision on her own.

She nodded slowly, then faster as she made up her mind. "Yes. Let's do this!"

"All right, it's a party!" Carlos jumped up from his seat. Mrs. Molina put a hand on his shoulder and pushed him back down.

"Not so fast." She cupped his cheek and looked across the table at her husband. "We'll need to see if Victoria can babysit tonight."

"And I need to change," Julie said, looking down at her giant dinosaur claw slippers. She scurried across the room, sliding on the polished wood floors while she ran up the stairs two at a time, leaving her nearly empty plate of pasta behind.

I pulled out my phone to text my parents about the last-minute change in plans. My dad would probably be disappointed—he'd wanted to watch a documentary about dolphins over a bowl of kale chips and warm cups of green tea, which under normal circumstances would have been fun. I loved hanging out with my parents . . . most of the time.

But Julie was about to sing onstage with her mom at the Dog Gone Lounge! I wouldn't miss that for anything.

"Does anyone know where my keys are?" Mr. Molina patted his pockets, looking around him for the one item he *always* lost.

"Check under the mail," Julie's mom said, looking completely unfazed. She popped the collar of her leather jacket, looking ready to fuel the fires of fierceness onstage. As soon as Julie came down, it was *on*.

This was gonna be one heck of a show.

1995

Luke

Last night, we were packed shoulder to shoulder in the Palace Theatre, watching the Foo Fighters rock out into the wee hours of the morning. Now we were at the Orpheum Theater, preparing for our own show. In the course of one day, we'd gone from being spectators of a show to *being* the show. I trembled with anticipation.

It couldn't get better than this.

Well—it *could*. I rubbed my throat, feeling the scratchiness brought on by this afternoon's exertions. I wished I'd heeded Alex's advice and not spent so much of my vocal cords on our street performance. Now I worried I wouldn't have my full voice by the time the curtains opened. And we still had sound check before

167

then. Ever the practical voice of the group, Alex had been right yet again.

I'd never tell him I said that, though.

"Excuse me?" I crossed the darkened theater, waving at a waitress wiping down tables. I pointed to the bar behind me. "Do you think I could get some hot tea? My throat is killing me."

"Oh, I'm not allowed behind the bar." She smiled awkwardly, tucking her hair behind her ear. "I'm not a bartender. You have to be twenty-one to do that, and I'm not quite that old yet."

I knew those rules were strict from my time working at the diner. When I needed to restock glasses, I handed them to an older employee over the counter, making sure not to put a toe behind the line. Otherwise, they could lose their business license.

"I totally understand. Thanks anyway." I ran my fingers through my hair and headed backstage, trying to clear my throat by coughing through the ache.

"Wait," the girl said from across the room. "I have an idea."

Leaning over the counter, she flipped a switch to turn on the hot water heater. She placed a mug beneath the faucet, then stretched her arm even farther to grab a tea bag from the tin on the other side. Her ribs strained against the chipped wood counter. She pulled back with a breathy groan just as the tin toppled to the ground with a *clank*.

"Whoopsies. Rose, you're such a klutz." She giggled as she held up a single tea bag. "But I got one!"

"Thank you, thank you, *thank you*," I said, running over to meet Rose by the bar. She tossed the tea into the mug and poured hot water over it. In that moment, she reminded me of my mom and how she used to take care of me whenever I got sick—the way she *always* took care of me. My heart panged at the thought of not having her here tonight, of not sharing this amazing day with her.

I shook my head, unwilling to get sucked into that train of thought. After our close call this afternoon, I was more determined than ever to make things right with my mom. I would go see her tomorrow, and hopefully that would be the start of everything getting better between us. My eyes refocused as I looked back to Rose, taking a small sip from my piping hot mug. "This is really hitting the spot. Thanks again."

"It's no problem. You sounded like you needed it." Rose leaned forward, whispering conspiratorially, "But if anyone asks, you didn't get that from me."

She winked and walked off, dragging the damp rag off her shoulder so that she could continue wiping down tables. Bobby joined me by the bar, watching Rose intently.

"I'm *definitely* going to try to get her number later," Bobby said in little more than a whisper as he watched the waitress retreat.

"Not if I can help it." Reggie nudged his side, also eyeing her. In an instant, his crush on the *Spin* intern from earlier this afternoon disappeared in a *poof.* He only had eyes for the curly-haired beauty.

"I saw her first." Bobby pushed off the counter, standing up straight. He stood head and shoulders above Reggie, and he was obviously trying to stake a claim.

What a bunch of amateurs.

"Guys, you can't call dibs on a *person.*" I bristled at the notion of them fighting over someone, especially since they hadn't even spoken to her. They weren't wrong to admire her—she was very nice to give me hot tea, even though she wasn't supposed to be behind the bar. And of course she was gorgeous with her long spiral curls reaching well below her shoulders. But she didn't deserve to be bickered over.

I wanted to tell them that there was *no way* they'd ever get girlfriends if they treated women like something to be conquered. Instead, I settled for their more obvious hurdle. "She's perfectly able to make her own decisions. Let her decide for herself—*after* the show. Okay?"

Bobby nodded with a cocky grin, clearly convinced that he would prevail. Reggie held his hands up, spinning around to walk in the opposite direction, viewing it as a deferred challenge.

Backstage was a maze of hallways that led to set staging areas, break rooms, and guest lounges. I wandered deeper into the bowels of the theater, passing our tiny green room, where Alex was thumping his drumsticks against the back of the couch—warming himself up for sound check. At the end of one of the halls was an emergency exit, propped open with a piece of wood wedged underneath the doorframe. I stepped out into the cool shade of an alleyway, my hot tea steaming into the wind. My footsteps echoed off the narrow pathway as I walked to the edge of the sidewalk.

The sun was already beginning to sink behind the Hollywood skyline, and the theater had finally turned on the neon lights of its iconic two-story sign. Now the blue and white lights of the Orpheum stared back at me, blinking with anticipation. Written on the marquee in big black letters was our band name.

SUNSET CURVE SHOWCASE—SOLD OUT.

"They're ready for us for sound check." Reggie leaned out the doorway, cupping his hand around his mouth so that I could hear him down the alley. "And when we're done, let's grab a quick bite before the show? We found some loose change underneath the couch cushions in our green room."

Count on Reggie to always be hungry.

"It'll have to be *super* cheap." I jogged over to meet him, sloshing warm tea over the rim of my mug in the process. We'd spent literally all our money on those T-shirts. We were flat broke.

"We'll figure something out. We always do!" Reggie skipped down the hall to gather the rest of the band. I took my time as I followed him, letting the hot tea soothe my throat. I knew it was just a sound check, but I wanted to blow it out of the water anyway.

Because tonight was *everything.*

21

Julie

Our car eased to a stop in front of the Dog Gone Lounge, a hole-in-the-wall, with a green awning covering a weathered redbrick façade. It was squished between a travel agency and a dimly lit alley, where workers were moving amps and black boxes into the back door of a theater. The entrance to the Lounge was on the other side of the block. A short line formed underneath the awning, as people waited to be seated in the small venue.

"Don't worry, we'll get seats. The place is bigger than it looks, and we're on the early side of the night," Dad said as he unlocked the car doors. He brought my mom's hand to his lips and gave it a soft kiss. "You go ahead while I find a parking spot. I'm not gonna pay a valet to do something I'm perfectly capable of."

Mom sighed as she reclaimed her hand. "Mi amor, last time it took you over half an hour to find a spot. It *is* a Saturday night in West Hollywood, after all."

"Yo lo sé." His grip tightened around the steering wheel. He had a thing about wasting money on valets. If he spent ten dollars on parking, he'd spend the rest of the night looking at the menu and pointing out all the things we could have bought with that money. He wouldn't budge on this; his mind was made up. "I've got this; don't worry."

"Okay, dear." Mom closed the door. Rapping on the backdoor window, she motioned for Flynn and me to come join her in line. "Let's leave Dad to his own devices. Come on, girls."

On the sidewalk, the city was alive. Hot dog and sandwich vendors sold their food down the block, and a bodega with every kind of newspaper stood to the side of the club's door. We settled into the short line, the third party to be seated. Flynn pressed her face against the glass and waved for me to join her.

"Jules, you've gotta see this." Her breath fogged up the glass.

I leaned in closer, looking at the circular coffee bar in the middle of the room and the mismatched couches and comfy armchairs scattered around the room. The lounge looked more like a coffee shop with a stage than an actual club. Now I understood why my parents were cool with me and Flynn tagging along.

"No way. I didn't know Trevor Wilson sang at the Dog Gone." Flynn pointed to the sun-bleached poster in the corner of the window. "Your parents are seriously cool to bring you here."

"I guess, but Carrie's dad is *way* cooler. I mean . . . *Trevor Wilson*! One of the greats," I said, thinking about all of Trevor's music. He inspired me to write my own songs. There was just something about his lyrics that called to me—that touched the very essence of my soul and spoke to me in a way nothing else did.

I used to talk to him about music whenever I went over to Carrie's house. But now that she'd basically stopped talking to me, that was over, too. My heart hiccupped. I knew I needed to accept that things between me and Carrie weren't going back to the way they were, but it still made me sad.

I breathed sharply, feeling a sudden wave of nerves rumble through my body. Her dad's music flooded into my head, great ballads I couldn't compete with. I couldn't stand on the same stage Trevor Wilson did.

"I don't know if I can do this," I said in a breathy whisper.

"What?" Flynn whipped her head around, her long braids flying in the air. "*Of course* you can do this."

"Okay, we're up. Let's go put our names on the list," Mom said over our gushed chatter. "I want them to call us before it gets too late."

"Can we stay out here?" I asked. I hadn't stepped forward when the line moved up, and there was a huge gap between us. I was frozen to the spot. "Just need to catch my breath."

Mom chewed on the side of her cheek as she thought about my request. She bent over so that she was at eye level with me. "You can stay outside for a little while longer *only* if you stay on this side of the block—and you two need to stick together."

Flynn and I nodded in agreement, but Mom lingered a few moments longer, obviously worried about leaving us on a busy LA street. But she trusted me enough to give me space, and that was exactly what I needed right now.

As soon as she disappeared into the Dog Gone Lounge, I took off down the sidewalk. The evening breeze was cool against my skin as I pushed the limits of my one-block radius. The patter of Flynn's shoes thumped behind me.

"Um, hello!" Flynn grabbed my shoulder, pulling

me to a halt. "Remember when we made a deal that we would always tell each other when we're standing in our own way?"

"Yeah," I said, looking down at the pavement instead of at Flynn's face.

"Well, duh. Hi. You're doing it again."

I knew what she was talking about. Over the summer, when I'd tried out for the super competitive music program at Los Feliz High School, no one was allowed in the auditorium to cheer me on. I couldn't lean on my mom or Flynn to give me strength. I was so nervous before the audition, I nearly threw up. Thankfully, I was accepted into the program, but I sometimes thought about how close I came to failing.

But this situation was different—performing my original music in front of a crowd of strangers in *Hollywood*. Stars had graced the stage of the Dog Gone. I wasn't on that level.

Right?

"Trevor Wilson sang there." I pointed down the block, where the line in front of the Lounge was growing longer. "I'm just a freshman who wrote a song with her mom. And I'm not even sure it's good.

"It *is* good—great even."

"We finished writing that song *months* ago and

haven't even practiced it." The blood drained from my face as I conjured up a horror image of what could happen tonight. "Oh my goodness, what if we get booed off the stage?!"

"Hey! Don't talk about my best friend like that." Flynn clapped her hands, snapping my attention back to the present. She gripped my shoulders with both of her hands. "Jules, *breathe*! Remember the day of your music program audition? Remember what I told you then?"

"Oh, you mean right after Carrie walked out of her audition looking smug and perfect?" I muttered under my breath, remembering standing in the hallway freaking out. Flynn was at my side, giving me a pep talk, and Carrie pushed through the doors of the auditorium, looking like she'd just gotten a perfect score from the faculty board. And even though we were *supposed to be* friends, she didn't even stop to wish me good luck, which had really rattled me. It was one of the first times I really realized how much our relationship had changed.

I wondered what would happen between us if we stopped being friends altogether. How would we act if we passed each other in the hallway at school? Would she keep ignoring me—or become my biggest competition?

"Ugh, forget about Carrie!" Flynn rattled my shoulders again. "She's *literally* just a miserable human who doesn't know how good she had it being your friend. It's not like she's your nemesis or enemy or whatever. But you know what? If she does turn out to be your enemy, then she'll be mine, too. Because the enemy of my friend is my . . . enemy? Wait how does that saying go?"

Flynn released her grip on my shoulders, frowning as she tried to remember the exact phrasing of the old adage.

"Flynn." I waved my hand in front of her distant stare. "Flynn! It doesn't matter—I get what you're trying to say."

"Come, on. What did I tell you before your audition?"

"You said: Strut onto the stage with *entitlement*, because while you're on it, you *own* it." Just saying those words gave me a jolt of confidence, just enough to turn my feet back in the direction of the Dog Gone Lounge's open mic night.

"Exactly. Go own that stage."

And then I walked arm in arm with one of my biggest cheerleaders.

22

Flynn

Mrs. Molina's eyes looked equal parts worried and relieved as they followed me and Julie through the coffee shop. We wove through the tightly packed crowd, shimmying through rows of couches and tattered armchairs until we got to the corner of the room where she'd saved us some seats.

Everything she owned was slung over the surrounding chairs—her jacket, her purse, a lone pair of reading glasses. Anything to make it seem like the seats were taken.

"You had me worried." She gripped Julie's arm. Her eyes were still tight with worry, but she smiled through it. She brought Julie in for a hug. Over her head, she looked to me, mouthing, "Thank you."

Aww, shucks.

I shook my head. It was nothing. I'd do anything for my best friend. And if that meant running down the block to stop her from running away from fate—so be it.

"I got some last-minute jitters, that's all." Julie took a deep breath and sank into one of the chairs.

"I get those *every time* I go up." Mrs. Molina scooted a chair closer to Julie, resting her hand on her knee. She rubbed her thumb against Julie's leg in small, soothing circles.

"Really?" I raised my eyebrows, surprised. I stepped closer to their conversation. "Don't you get onstage regularly?"

"I'm only human." She shrugged. "The nerves and adrenaline are normal—they let you know you're *alive*. Never let that stop you from getting onstage. Lean into it, not away from it."

"Any tips and tricks?" Julie asked, leaning closer, clearly interested in how to up her game.

"I picture mi abuela. I know it sounds weird because she's gone. But I imagine that if I sing loudly enough, if I sing with enough conviction, she can hear me all the way on the other side, wherever she may be." Her eyes glazed over, like she was thinking about her grandmother now. She shook her head, returning her gaze to us. "Sometimes I think about singing to your father. You can pick *anyone* to sing to. And when you are singing to that loved one, the audience sort of melts away. And it's just the song that carries you."

As if Mr. Molina could feel his wife's pull, he swung open the door to the Lounge and scanned the crowd, locking eyes with her as soon as he spotted our little corner. In his piercing gaze, I caught notes of adoration and love. I looked away, giving them their private moment.

He wove through the crowd, only breaking eye contact with Mrs. Molina long enough to look where he was stepping. When he reached us, he wiped his forehead in mock relief.

"See, I told you no worries," he huffed, clearly still out of breath from wherever he'd parked the car. He looked at his watch, smiling at the time. "That only took twenty minutes. I'm getting better at this."

Julie laughed and shook her head. But Mr. Molina didn't notice—he'd locked eyes with Rose again. He wrapped his arm around her waist.

"Ay, mi amor." He kissed her cheek, lingering *slightly* too long. "I forgot how much I *love* that leather jacket." He lowered his voice, leaning closer to her ear.

"Remember that time we went to Las Vegas and you got up onstage and—"

"Um, *hello*? You have company." Julie pointed her finger at her chest, then at me. "This is supposed to be date night *lite*, okay?"

I cleared my throat, not even thinking about mentioning the heart eyes her dad had made across the room. I'd keep that one to myself. Mrs. Molina squeezed Julie's chin and wiggled her nose playfully.

"Right. We'll talk about Vegas later. Where did you stash the car this time?" Julie's mom raised her eyebrows toward her husband, her eyes alight with amusement.

"Eh." He bobbed his head side to side, avoiding her intent gaze. "It's tucked safely away behind a shopping center cargo bay. It's fine." He held his hands up in defense. "We won't get towed."

He slid Mrs. Molina's sheet music across the table with a wink. "You don't want to forget this up there, do you?"

"All right," the emcee boomed as he hopped onto the stage. He peered down at the clipboard in his hands. "Next up on the list is Dos Dahlias."

Ohmigod, cutest name ever, right?

"You ready to sing to your person?" Rose Molina held her hand to her daughter.

"Can my person be *you*?" Julie asked from her chair, frozen to the spot.

I watched intently, curious to know if her advice worked even when the person you were singing to was on the *same stage*.

"Of course it can, mija." She grinned, her eyes growing bright. Julie grabbed her hand without hesitation and her mom drew her in for a tight hug. "Come on. Let's sing to each other."

The emcee handed both of them microphones. Julie held hers in her hands, and she smiled awkwardly as Mrs. Molina slid onto the bench behind the keyboard onstage, adjusting her mic in the attached mic stand. I shouted before the music started, "Woo! Go, Team Molina!"

Julie and her mom smiled warmly at each other, and then, with her fingers poised on the keys, Mrs. Molina nodded her head, mouthing down her countdown.

Then she started playing—a soft thrumming intro before her lips found the mic.

My love, mi corazón, my heart
So much to say, but where to start
I dreamed of you expectantly
Now you're real, perfect, and lovely

I gave you life—it's not enough
'Cause life is hard, the road is tough
Find your strength, and know your power
Never let them see you cower

Julie rushed across the stage, commanding it like I *knew* she could. She sidled up to the keyboard, her brown curly mane swinging behind her as she swayed to her mom's instrumentals. She threw her head back, raising her mic in the air, and joined her mom on the chorus.

So fuel the fires of fierceness
Cast out the shadow of weakness
Hold your head up high and you'll find
A fire inside you can't deny

Light a spark and watch the flames
Brighten the darkness and light the way
My dear, mi corazón
You were born to slay!

Julie took a deep breath before launching into her verses.

Mami, you're here, my guiding star
I am who I am because of what you are

Looking at you, here's what I see
Talent refined, what I hope to be

A beam of light to see me through
All that I'm destined to be I see in you
So very different, yet so much the same
Searching for meaning while chasing the flame

Rose picked up the tempo of her piano accompaniment, lifting the song to new heights. She leaned forward to join Julie for the last few verses.

'Cause we're very different, yet so much the same
Searching for meaning while chasing the flame
We're better together than working alone
Ablaze with the fire in our bones

We're fueling the fire of fierceness
My dear, you're wired for greatness
Hold your head up high and you'll find
A fire inside you can't deny

Light a spark and watch the flames
Brighten the darkness and light the way
My dear, mi corazón
You were born to slay!

23

Julie

My voice trailed off as the memory of that perfect day faded into the back of my mind. It was kind of amazing that my two favorite memories both revolved around me doing a live performance, especially considering how they used to kinda freak me out. But now, every time I took the stage with my own music, I got a little less nervous—especially with my phantoms standing beside me.

My mom had told me to hold a person in my heart while I performed—that if I sang loudly and with enough conviction, that person could hear me all the way on the other side, wherever they may be.

Tonight onstage at the Orpheum, just like I did on our perfect day together, I'd sung to my mom. And I *knew* she heard me. Because if anyone could figure out how to get messages in the great beyond, it was Rose Molina.

The chairs on the studio ceiling dangled above our heads, a testament to how creative my mom could be. I lay there, feeling a tear travel slowly down my cheek. Luke wiped it away with a swipe of his finger, causing me to jump. I'd almost forgotten that we could touch— for now, anyway.

"Don't cry," he said, rubbing my tear between his fingers. "These are happy memories, remember?"

"I *am* happy, but it's complicated. It wasn't long after our show at the Dog Gone Lounge that we found out my mom was sick. And then she was *really sick*, and then she was just . . . gone," I said in a low voice. "I thought I'd never have a perfect day again—until we played tonight."

I sniffled into the back of my palm. "Thanks for reminding me of that day. I love talking about my mom. I never want to forget her, you know? I always want to be able to close my eyes and see her face."

"I know what you mean." He nodded solemnly, and I knew he meant what he said. Luke spoke to me in a way that cut through all my layers and went straight to the heart. He raised his hand, pointing to the chairs above. "I'd been wondering who hung those."

"You've never seen chairs on a ceiling before? Weird."
I chuckled, my nose a little stuffy from all the tears.

"It's not something you see every day—equal parts
beautiful and mysterious."

I rolled to my side and found him looking straight
at me. He wasn't looking at the chairs on the ceiling at
all. His eyes were only on me. Did he mean *I* was
beautiful?

Omigod!

Blinking away from his gaze, I heaved myself into a
standing position and walked over to the couch. For the
second time tonight, I felt the need to put some distance
between me and the crackling feeling that surrounded
me and Luke. I sat on the couch, figuring I was at a
safe distance.

Luke's eyes were bright as he popped off the palette
of cushions. He walked slowly to my side of the room,
choosing to sit on the arm of the couch instead of right
next to me.

See? Luke knows me so well.

"I can't believe you played at the Dog Gone
Lounge." He shook his head, his eyes full of the same
wonder they'd had since we performed tonight. "And
you've played the Orpheum, too? What are you—some
kind of living legend?"

"You are, too." I blushed, looking away, afraid I touched a sensitive subject. Luke wasn't exactly alive, but he wasn't *gone* either. "Well, kind of."

"I *feel* alive. Caleb's curse is finally in our rearview mirror. It's another brave new world." He leaned over the edge of the couch, looking at me through his impossibly long lashes. "You know? I only know one other person who's played those two venues under the age of eighteen."

"Who?"

His eyes locked on mine, making my cheeks grow hot. "Me."

How is it possible Luke gets cuter every time I look at him?

"The Dog Gone is *right* around the block from the diner where I worked, so I used to pop over during my lunch breaks and play a song—sometimes two. Just to play, you know? It was during the middle of the day when literally no one was watching. Except one day, there was an agent there." He sighed, sinking onto the couch. Only one cushion separated us. "She gave me her card and told me to call her when the band played a bigger venue. I thought it was the coolest piece of paper I'd ever seen.

"Once we pulled in every favor we had to get the gig at the Orpheum, we invited her to the show. That was one of the first times I thought, *Wow, this could* really *happen*."

"And you finally lived your dream tonight." I nodded, scooting over. I couldn't help it. I felt so acutely drawn to him.

"I wish I'd spoken to my mom that day, though." He'd dropped his voice to little more than a whisper, but I could still hear that the words were laced with pain.

"That must have been rough to remember."

"Nah." He shrugged, wiping away a tear on his arm. "I mean, it stings a little."

"I know how you feel. When I think about singing at the Dog Gone, that day was so wonderful. But looking back, thinking about *her* . . ." I closed my eyes, seeing my mother's face again.

I did know exactly how he felt. Not just because I'd read the gut-wrenching lyrics of his song "Unsaid Emily," but because I did the same thing. I thought about my mom almost every day, and I wished I could talk to her. "It gets me sometimes."

Tonight at the Orpheum, I couldn't stop thinking about the advice she'd given to me just before we'd gone onstage for our final show together. When I'd walked onto that platform by myself, feeling the stage lights boring into me, my stomach had filled with nerves, and adrenaline surged through my veins. They were the same jitters I'd felt at the Dog Gone.

Even though I'd been tempted to run, I'd held my mom's advice in my heart and leaned into my nerves, just like she'd suggested.

And I sang to her.

"You're thinking about her right now, aren't you?" Luke whispered. He scooted closer, closing the final gap between us.

"Yeah," I said with a sniffle. But looking at his face, something made me laugh. "What are *you* thinking about?"

"I still get a kick out of the fact that you love Trevor Wilson's songs."

"Uh, get over it already," I said, knowing *exactly* where he was going with this. "Yes, I like *your* songs. I admit it!" I covered my face with my hands to hide my blush.

He pumped his fist in the air, clearly pleased with himself. His face softened, and he leaned forward. "I like you, too."

I wanted to say I liked him back, but I was *literally* paralyzed. He had that effect on me. We sat in silence for a while, just happy to be in each other's company. I tilted my head, suddenly remembering something he'd said earlier.

"Do you think your pact with Alex and Reggie had anything to do with you guys coming back here?" On Luke's last day alive, he'd made a toast with the rest of the band, promising to always come back to the studio, to always hold this place dear. Maybe they'd forged a permanent connection or something, and it wasn't unfinished business keeping them here—maybe they were collectively keeping one another tied to this place.

"I don't know if we have that much power. Maybe?" He hiked his leg onto the couch, turning to face me. He held out his pinkie. "Let's make a pact now—you and me—to keep writing songs together, here in this studio."

"You've got yourself a deal." I gripped his pinkie with mine, squeezing it tightly. I wasn't sure how long this would all last and I had no idea how much all our lives were about to change—but for now, I wanted as much of my phantom as I could get.

ABOUT THE AUTHOR

Photo credit: Clementine Cayrol

Candace Buford has been an avid reader since childhood—always looking for stories with strong and complex POCs. She graduated from Duke University with a degree in German literature, which exposed her to the delightfully creepy side of storytelling by writers like Kafka and Brecht. She also holds a law degree from Penn State Law School and a business degree from Duke's Fuqua School of Business. Raised in Houston, Candace currently lives in the heart of Seattle, where you can find her huddled in café corners, scribbling away in her notebook. She shares her life with a rocket scientist and a Plott Hound, who both ensure there is never a dull day. She is also the author of *Kneel*.